John Ward

The Overland Route to California

And other Poems

John Ward

The Overland Route to California
And other Poems

ISBN/EAN: 9783744791915

Printed in Europe, USA, Canada, Australia, Japan

Cover: Foto ©Andreas Hilbeck / pixelio.de

More available books at **www.hansebooks.com**

THE

OVERLAND ROUTE

TO

CALIFORNIA,

AND OTHER POEMS.

BY JOHN WARD.

NEW YORK.

1875.

CONTENTS.

iv.

TO

MY COMPANIONS

ON THE

OVERLAND ROUTE.

A SOUVENIR

OF

A PLEASANT JOURNEY.

THE OVERLAND ROUTE.

THE JOURNEY.

I.

We are gliding swift away to the grand Pacific shore :
  And the prairies stretch afar their boundless sweep :
Mississippi's mighty tide, and a hundred rivers more.
  Watch our course to yonder Rocky-Mountain steep.

II.

Council Bluffs in beauty rise by the dark Missouri's wave :
  Like sceptred king enthroned, each noble hill :
Fair Nebraska stretches wild, where so late the Indian brave
  Shot the bison by the prairie's sparkling rill.

7

III.

The bluffs recede from view, and the Platte's unbending flow
  Bounds the verdant plain's expanse of virgin mould;
Where alone the cotton tree skirts the river's current free:
  And of yore, untamed, the prairie fires rolled.

IV.

The sunset fires the sky with a glow of golden haze,
  While horsemen urge the roving cattle home;
Then Pawnees view our flight, wondering still, in dull amaze,
  What fiend invades the regions where they roam.

V.

When the morning light returns, with the cooling, western breeze.
  The prairie-dogs leap up on many a mound;
The antelope comes swift o'er the plain unknown to trees,
  Where soldiers guard the Indians' hunting-ground.

THE JOURNEY.

VI.

That range of rounding hills marks the nearing mountain-gate ;
    But we miss the shaggy herds of grazing kine :
Where countless thousands roamed, came the tireless hand of Fate,
    And Indians for the chase in vain repine.

VII.

Like storm clouds from the main, soars the Colorado chain,
    Giant peaks enwrapped in robes of snowy white,
With majestic mien and glance, pointing, each with icy lance,
    To the calm that reigns in skies supremely bright.

VIII.

The mountain breezes sweep through the valleys as we rise,
    While the prairie monarch flies to quiet dales :
Surging hills, like ocean crests, frown beneath the tranquil skies,
    Rifted by the dreamy slopes of endless vales.

9

IX.

We scale a towering range of the Rocky-Mountain heights,
  With a slow, increasing rise from mile to mile;
The lingering snows attest how we soar with eagle flights,
  Till on yonder lofty crest we pause awhile.

X.

Onward! down the giddy steep with a curving, gradual sweep,
  Through the ruddy granite portals on we glide:
While the Northern snowy peaks, as we near the Western deep,
  Tell the grand Sierras whither swift we ride.

XI.

The cool Nebraska winds to the far Sweet Water land:
  We watch her current's clear and tranquil flow;
Yon mounds resemble walls reared to guard a warrior band,
  And purple mountains catch the sunset glow.

XII.

Herds of antelopes speed on, as the day draws near its close,
  And the prairie wolf surveys the throng in vain;
Then a shower of golden light glows above the distant snows,
  And the evening's silvery cressets gleam again.

XIII.

Rising over many a height, when the early morning light
  Wakes thought again from dreaming fancy's chain,
By the Uintah range we go, crowned with shining crests of snow,
  And pass the wilds of many a desert plain.

XIV.

Yon dark Shoshonee braves on the war-path seek the foe,
  Where battle fierce may soon enchant their eyes:
While noble Washakie stands a chieftain proud and free,
  And the mounted squaw protects her infant prize.

11

XV.

Amid the native tribes gaze the children of the Sun,
  The almond-eyed Mongolians' ancient race:
They laid the magic rail; spanned the torrents one by one;
  But long their roving footsteps to retrace.

XVI.

Here the Mormon Prophet stood on that rocky pulpit's stair,
  And preached to raptured multitudes below,
Where Echo Cañon's weird, fantastic cliffs breathe in the air
  That sweeps from yonder pinnacles of snow.

XVII.

Down the Weber Cañon's bends, by her river's rapid tide,
  To the beauteous vale below we swiftly speed,
Where verdant hills uprise to the rugged mountain's side,
  And many a rill divides the grassy mead.

12

THE JOURNEY.

XVIII.

By the long and snowy range; o'er the Weber's quickening stream,
  As it storms the Devil's Gate in rapids grand;—
Down to smiling plains beneath, where the Mormon's mystic dream
  Turns the desert to a lovely, fertile land.

XIX.

Apollo's radiant bow wings its flaming darts below,
  That gild the vale where steeds of Commerce meet:
Sentry summits proudly stand, circling round the enchanted land,
  And clearest air brings near their rocky feet.

XX.

While the day-star seeks the West, to the inland sea we haste,
  Where the salt-breeze wafts the duck and curlew's flight;
Like snow-fields stretch the plains where the lake has left the waste,
  And the mountain chain shades dark the Sabbath night.

XXI.

O'er Nevada's arid plain, in a misty, driving rain,
　　With the morning light, we swiftly speed our course;
While the merry gnomes below veil their treasures with the snow.
　　Where golden veins wind round their mountain source.

XXII.

Again the radiant sun blazes o'er the waste amain,
　　And the breeze, as though impelled by Afrite's power,
Blows the desert dust in clouds o'er the wild, uncanny plain,
　　Where rugged hills in sullen masses tower.

XXIII.

The crimson streamers gleam, as the day fades like a dream,
　　And night's dark shadows dim the twilight's peace:
Then comes a cooling air from the Western regions fair:
　　There grand Sierras rise, and deserts cease.

14

XXIV.

With the early steps of day, by an endless, covered way,
  O'er high Sierra's forest slope we go ;
Through countless rifts, the light flames like rockets in the night,
  And morning beams illume the shining snow.

XXV.

Have the Titans reared this ledge? and have fairies set that hedge
  Amid the Ice King's realms of endless cold ?
Look adown this fearful steep ! where the rapid torrents leap,
  Bearing on to distant valleys flakes of gold.

XXVI.

How sublime the verdant scene ! as we glide the groves between,
  Hovering o'er the deep abyss that yawns below :
Then, beside the wondrous mines, on we rush through lofty pines
  Down the dizzy steeps to westward slopes aglow.

15

THE OVERLAND ROUTE.

XXVII.

Sacramento's waving sheaves, where the fig-tree's sombre leaves
    Amid the oak-trees catch the passer's eye,
With fertile fields and plains, all declare, that Freedom reigns
    Beneath the snowy peaks that cloud the sky.

XXVIII.

Like the vastness of the deep, the wheat-fields' ripening sweep
    Stretches wide, as rippling breezes bow the grain;
While the stately live-oaks rise, waving greetings from the skies,
    Where whirling sails draw moisture to the plain.

XXIX.

By foaming rivers wide,—for the snows have swelled their tide;
    Across the Coast Sierra's mountain-way;
We scent the ocean breeze from the ever-nearing seas:
    A world of fairy lights gleams o'er the bay!

16

CALIFORNIA.

I.

Beneath a mountain's towering steep
  A mighty ocean rolls,
Awakening, with the boundless sweep
And echoing thunders of its deep,
  Strange visions in our souls.

II.

The great sea-lions sportive play
  Amid the eddying foam;
With bellowing roar they cleave the spray,
Or bask in sunshine all the day
  Around their rocky home.

17

III.

'T is not the dark Atlantic's wave
  That crests the craggy shore.
Where giant breakers foaming rave,
And naught yon hapless bark could save
  Amid their awful roar.

IV.

Is this the sea for calmness famed,
  Pacific's tranquil main?
These glorious waves were never tamed,
And falsely is the ocean named
  That breasts yon sandy plain!

V.

But awful grandeur all is thine,
  Majestic, Western sea!
Whose whitening breakers frost the brine
In rolling sweep and endless line
  Of wild sublimity!———

CALIFORNIA.

VI.

Then hail, as sinks the sun to rest,
  A valley, grand and wild,
Where Nature seems to strive her best
To crown the fair Pacific West,
  As though her favorite child!

VII.

Yosemite in splendor sleeps,
  With leafy groves and bowers;
While, from the lofty, rocky steeps,
The cataracts, in mighty leaps,
  Sweep down to vales of flowers.

VIII.

'T is Eden given back to Earth,
  In beauty all its own!
Too fair for aught of mortal birth:
Too solemn for a mortal's mirth;
  The gem of our fair zone!

19

IX.

Its towering cliffs and verdant meads
  Are domed by azure skies,
That smile as though Arcadian reeds
Were piped around, and warlike deeds
  Had ne'er sought valor's prize.

X.

The rocky shaft El Capitan
  Shoots up beside the vale
In startling grandeur; daring man
To climb where never mortal can,
  And braving every gale !

XI.

The waving spray, from falls too high
  For aught but eagles' flight,
Sends misty showers, as from the sky,
While rainbow-tints in radiance vie
  Beneath yon lofty height.

XII.

Sublimity of rock and fall,
 With towering, granite peaks
Enchased in bowers and forests tall;
Fair valley, 't is enchantment all
 That from thy beauty speaks!

XIII.

Colossal columns mount supreme,
 As though the Genii's might
Had reared a temple; that would seem
A wonderful, immortal dream
 Of brilliant realms of light!

XIV.

Here, Titan brothers three arise,
 In crests of diamond form;
There, swift as meteor from the skies,
A cataract, in silvery guise,
 Resounds like coming storm.

21

XV.

These massive crags were rent, perchance,
   By fierce, volcanic fires,
In early years of Time's advance,
Till Heaven's frosts and sunbeam-glance
   Have shaped cathedral spires.

XVI.

You domes of granite, parted now,
   A solemn, stately pair,
May once have touched, with lordly brow,
Where glades extend with verdant bough,
   Kissed by the summer air.

XVII.

The mountains watch the clear Merced,
   That mirrors glories rare,
As, lifting high each sovereign head,
These rocky marvels rise to wed
   The tempest in its lair!

22

CALIFORNIA.

XVIII.

But climb, by yonder sister falls,
　　To dizzy crests of snow,
Where all that tranquil souls appals
Sublimely reigns, in Terror's halls,
　　While danger lurks below!

XIX.

In mighty curves, the snowy peaks
　　Sweep round our vantage place;
Where, throned on clouds in stormy weeks,
The rolling thunder threatening speaks
　　When Nature veils her face.

XX.

From heights like these, defying time,
　　And crowned with frosty wreath,
That valley grand, of genial clime.
A chasm seems in crags sublime,
　　Whose domes rise far beneath.

23

XXI.

O grand Sierra!   Alpine crests,
  And wondrous vales below,
Are what fair Nature's pilgrim guests,
With beating hearts and heaving breasts,
  Behold amid thy snow!

XXII.

That deep, precipitous abyss,
  With waving forests clad,
Leads down to fairy bowers of bliss,
More beauteous, far, than scenes like this,
  Where Nature scarce seems glad!

XXIII.

The Mercéd leaps, with thundering roar
  And clouds of dazzling spray,
By Broderick's summit, bleak and hoar:
Then dashes o'er yon rocky floor
  To blooming vales away;

24

XXIV.

Till, rainbow-wreathed, the river falls
 A sheet of sparkling foam,
In glorious plunge from rocky walls,
While every mighty cliff recalls
 Her rapids' mountain home.

XXV.

But with a gentler flow she pours
 Amid the oak-trees green,
Where many a pine majestic soars,
As if 't would rise to Heavenly doors,
 The stately groves between.

XXVI.

Then turn we to thy lovely glades,
 Yosemite, the fair!
Whose glossy foliage never fades,
Though storms may sweep from mountain shades.
 And floods may cloud the air.

XXVII.

O awful summits, rising high
From out this charming scene
In giant grandeur toward the sky!
Your massive, Alpine majesty
Is of celestial mien!

XXVIII.

Like seraph guards, your glittering walls
Surround this wondrous vale,
In stately towers and caverned halls,
And rocks that, 'mid the water-falls,
Seem crests and coats of mail!

XXIX.

Majestic guardians, vast and grand!
Your panoplied array
Protects a wild, mysterious land,
Where verdure decks the glistening sand,
And rushing rivers play.

CALIFORNIA.

XXX.

Sublimity and beauty fair
    Were never so combined,
Since first the ambient, summer air,
In Eden, fanned the primal pair,
    For Paradise designed!———

XXXI.

Through stately groves of towering pines:
    By cañons, deep and green:
O'er dreary plains—at length the signs
Of delving deep for golden mines
    'Mid rugged rocks are seen.

XXXII.

What powers have rent the earth in twain?
    What fissures scar the ground!
Misshapen rocks deform the plain,
As though the enchantress Circe's reign
    Had modern victims found!

27

XXXIII.

But yonder towers a mighty grove
    Of forest columns high.
Where giants might delight to rove,
Or find, if with great Jove they strove,
    Brave arms to dare the sky!

XXXIV.

Along a purling streamlet's course,
    Between encircling hills,
These wondrous trees have braved the force
Of Time, whose stroke, without remorse,
    Their stateliest rival kills.

XXXV.

Majestic monarchs of the soil,
    Of matchless height and girth!
Aspiring man's unceasing toil
The centuries have learned to foil,
    While still ye grace the earth!

28

CALIFORNIA.

XXXVI.

In stalwart hundreds grouped, ye stand,
  With lordly bough and limb :
As yet preserved from ruffian hand,
Like Lebanon's fair cedars grand,
  Ye breathe a silent hymn !

XXXVII.

While loftier than the carven spire
  Your shafts mount up in power,
With densest bark, scarce touched by fire :
Ye stand the oldest living choir
  That greets this gracious hour !———

XXXVIII.

Now view the bright, imposing scene,
  So near the Golden Gate,
Where California's Ocean Queen
Superbly reigns, with haughty mien,
  And knows no fear of Fate !

29

XXXIX.

The treasures of the East and West
  Adorn the princely town ;
Where generous feeling rules the best,
And cooling breezes soothe to rest
  The sharpest cynic's frown.

XL.

The mighty bay, where fleets may ride,
  With countless masts, secure,
Admits the vast Pacific's tide
Through mountain portals, deep and wide,
  By frowning guns made sure.

XLI.

Beyond the wondrous Golden Gate
  Are vales of softer skies :
There Tamalpaïs rears in state
Its rocky crest, while gales abate
  Their sweep, and zephyrs rise.

CALIFORNIA.

XLII.

San Rafael's clustering villas lie
  Amid the circling hills,
Where ranches reach the mountains high,
While over all, in majesty,
  Yon come the fancy fills.

XLIII.

A watch-tower of the skies it seems,
  A royal signal height,
To catch the morning's earliest beams,
And send them to the dancing streams.
  That hail the dawning light!

XLIV.

The groves on its volcanic side,
  Like velvet's softest pile,
In emerald verdure, serve to hide
Where once has flowed the fiery tide,
  Perchance, for many a mile.

31

XLV.

Then float across the noble bay
  To San Francisco's heights :
Where Chinese costumes, quaint and gay,
As though in Prince Aladdin's day,
  Recall Arabian Nights.

XLVI.

Or view them on the mimic stage,
  Fantastic as a dream,
While courts are held, and battles rage,
And Emperors, of a by-gone age,
  By rebels vanquished seem.

XLVII.

Imperial Pacific shore,
  What glorious future thine !
Atlantic empires' priceless lore,
With Chinese learning's ancient store,
  All crown thy work divine !

THE OVERLAND ROUTE.

`

THE RETURN.

I.

To Sacramento's strong levees,
   The bulwark of her pride,
We swiftly speed, where foaming seas
Have madly dashed among the trees
   From yonder river's tide.

II.

Again the grand Sierras rise,
   As o'er the heights we glide :
Though soon will dark, tempestuous skies
O'erwhelm the road in torrents' guise,
   Till havoc rages wide.

33

III.

Across the endless desert plain,
  We near the inland sea,
Whose islands sweep in mountain-chain,
Along the salt waves of its main,
  A stately company.

IV.

The Mormon City stretches fair
  On plains beyond the lake,
That, rising slow, may bid it share
The fate Lot's city seemed to dare,
  If vengeance should awake.

V.

From Utah lake, the Jordan clear,
  In fresh, delightful stream,
Pours down to swell yon bitter mere,
Whose lifeless waves are never drear,
  So brightly blue they seem.

THE RETURN.

VI.

The Wasatch Range and Oquirrh Hills
   Surround the fertile fields,
Where sparkle countless, merry rills,
Whose current yonder city fills
   With trees her soil ne'er yields.

VII.

That range of snowy mountains grand,
   Magnificent in sweep,
Is rich with mines, where Nature's hand
Has hidden, in the rock and sand,
   Her silvery treasures deep.

VIII.

On frowning heights, the Federal guns
   Command the sullen town :
The white tents gleam ; as setting suns,
Like molten gold that glittering runs,
   'Mid gorgeous clouds sink down.

35

IX.

A meteor flashes through the air
  With emerald light and glow ;
Now fading, now with dazzling glare,
It gleams across the twilight fair
  By yonder peaks of snow.

X.

From smiling fields, and salt morass,
  We thread the cañons steep,
Then soon, o'er many a mountain pass
And plains of sage, admire the grass
  Where deer may browse and leap.

XI.

At wild Cheyenne, a swarthy band
  Of chieftains mount the train,
To view their great White Father's land,
And tread the far Atlantic strand
  In painted pomp, again.

XII.

Missouri's current, dark and swift,
  Where down the mighty stream,
By verdant bluffs, with busy thrift,
The boats are swept in arrowy drift,
  Is soon a treasured dream.

XIII.

O'er Iowa's delightful meads,--
  What vision glances bright ?
Great Mississippi grandly speeds
'Mid fairy isles, nor, proudly, heeds
  The piers that brave its might.

XIV.

Through endless prairie corn-fields green,
  A city looms afar,
Arising with undaunted mien,
Her miles of ruin all between,
  A radiant, Western star !

37

XV.

What groans of anguish echoed late,
  When strong men, in despair,
Beheld the pride of earthly state,
With all that made their city great,
  Flame in the fiery air!

XVI.

Then, domes and towers, rocking slow,
  Were wrapped in seas of fire;
Then, echoed many a wail of woe,
As hurricanes of torrid glow
  O'erwhelmed the blazing spire.

XVII.

While ran a sympathetic thrill
  Of pity through the land
For homeless thousands, mourning still
The Fire King's imperious will,
  The world ne'er seemed so grand.

XVIII.

How nobly other lands averred
　　Their brotherhood the while,
Till, winged again, the city stirred,
Arising, like the wondrous bird,
　　From out her funeral pile !

XIX.

By Michigan's enchanting lake —
　　A pure and glorious sea —
We soon behold, while stars awake,
The silver moon her pathway take
　　In cloudless majesty :

XX.

We hail thy beauty, fairest Queen,
　　And greet thy argent light
That beams in tender, trembling sheen
Along the waves, that glow between
　　The steps of dreamy Night !

XXI.

Oh, when within the distant vale
  Whose splendors all sublime
Sweet dreams of Paradise exhale,
Could we have viewed thy glories pale,
  Too raptured were the time!

XXII.

The morning light invites our stay
  To roam the forest town,
Where stretch the brilliant villas gay
Through many a lovely, elm-grown way,-
  Lake Erie's verdant crown.

XXIII.

While soon the festal course is gained
  Where pant the rapid steeds,
By skilful training, deftly reined
Beyond Apollo's horses—feigned
  To tread celestial meads.

40

THE RETURN.

XXIV.

The lake, that Perry's valor gave
    A fame beyond its own,
All tranquil sleeps, though yonder wave
Of silvery peace ere long may brave
    Niagara's proud throne.

XXV.

Farewell, ye mighty lakes sublime!
    Your waters seaward roll,
And thither becks the hand of Time,
Our magic steed must seek the clime
    Where smiles a cherished goal!

XXVI.

We welcome thee, imperial State!
    Thy grandeur gilds the town
Where Genesee, by cruel fate,
No longer floods her rocky gate,
    Nor, foaming, plunges down.

XXVII.

While evening shadows watch our course
  To Hudson's lordly flow,
On fiery wings, the iron horse,
With speed as of enchanted force,
  O'er fertile plains shall go:

XXVIII.

Till early day adorns its reign,
  And brings the welcome breeze,
That, sweeping from the Atlantic's main,
Shall whisper: Home is near again,
  Manhattan by the seas!

THE UNDINE.

I.

An Undine sighed in her grot of shell,
And tear-drops from her bright eyes fell:
" Alas!" she cried, "no sympathy
Endears the creatures of the sea;
  Too cold our chilly blood
Pours its pallid stream along;
Loving friends to earth belong,
  Unknown beneath our flood!

II.

"I weary of gems and jewels rare,
And ceaseless pastime brings but care;
Slowly beats an Undine's heart,
Dead to love's bewitching art:
　　Yet why glows my cheek?
Why this pleasing, strange distress?
Love may not an Undine bless,
　　Born in caverns bleak!"

III.

Sang the Undine 'neath the tide:
"Would I were a mortal's bride!
Dwelling near some lovely lake:
Sporting in the tangled brake;
　　Free to cherish love:
Crowns of pearls I'd cast away;
Happy, leave the rainbow's play.
　　Meek as mating dove!"

44

IV.

All innocent of mortal guile
She sang, and struck her harp the while.
Widely echoed words like these.
Borne abroad by listening seas.
    Heard with proud disdain,
Roused her sisters' haughty pride:
" Leave," they cried, "our tranquil tide?
    Leave thy native main?

V.

" Sister, rove with us the deep ;
    Rouse the dolphin from his sleep!
    What is love? and what is man?
    Haste. forget thy foolish plan !
        What to us is earth?
    Dwelt the Undines here ere land
    Raised its head, or yet the strand
        Bound the ocean's girth ! "

THE UNDINE.

VI.

The Undine floated o'er the sea,
Harping sweetest minstrelsy ;
Sailors listened to her song
As she drew their bark along,
    Playing merrily
Round the prow and bulwarks brave,
Foaming in the swelling wave
    On the vessel's lee.

VII.

Her golden locks were wreathed with spray.
And, won by her enchanting lay,
A crowd of finny creatures came ;
The shark, whom only she could tame,
    Swam gently by her side :
The fishes love the fair Undine,
And will obey no other queen,
    For music rules the tide.

46

VIII.

A fisher-bark came sweeping by :
The Undine heaved a piteous sigh ;
And when she saw the crew prepare
Their fatal nets with cruel care,
  She struck her harp again ;
Oh ! wildly swelled the warning song :
"Ye fishers, do the fish no wrong,
  Or bid adieu to men ! "

IX.

The greedy nets are spreading free,
And drink the briny, rolling sea ;
But, charging fierce in loyal ranks,
The swordfish thrust through oaken planks ;
  The whale, with furious sweep,
Attacks the vessel's laboring keel :
The timbers crack ; the top-masts reel ;—
  She founders in the deep !

THE UNDINE.

X.

A wail is heard from yonder shore,
Where widowed wives, a saddened score,
Lament the fisher-bark in vain ;
Their sorrow gave the Undine pain :
    " Too cold am I! " she cried,
" I thought of my poor fish, alone,
And heeded not the swimmer's groan
    Who perished in the tide!

XI.

" Amid the breakers will I dwell,
And warn the sailor, by the swell
Of music rare, and echoes sweet,
That every note shall soft repeat,
    To fly from dangers hid ;
Then sweet shall be my balmy rest,
Pillowed upon the Ocean's breast,
    While sea-birds heed my bid! "

48

XII.

When breakers roar, and raves the blast,
The sailor, on the giddy mast,
Has often heard a cadence wild,
With words of warning, soft and mild,
    To steer a safer course:
The Undine, singing, becks away,
And leads, by dolphins' winning play,
    From tempests howling hoarse.

LADY GRACE'S BRIDAL.

I.

A castle beams in the ruddy light
  Of a thousand torches' blaze;
The moon looks calmly on the night,
Though warriors soon will rush to fight,
In festive mantles gaily dight,
  And filled with strange amaze.

II.

A lady's bower is yonder tower,
  Where knotted rope is seen
To wave in the kiss of the evening breeze,
That shakes the vines on a sculptured frieze:
It hangs from a window hid by trees,
  But gleams in Dian's sheen.

III.

In raftered hall, where feasted all,
   There gathered many a dame
In gay attire. A bridal scene!
See Lady Grace, in beauty, lean
On a husband's arm, of princely mien
   And proud, ancestral name!

IV.

At maiden's call, she left the hall;
   A dizziness, 't was said,
Had seized her as the priest said grace:
She whispered, with a blushing face,
'T would soon be past; with modest pace
   Then left the table's head.

V.

The baron smiled, yet blamed his child,
    While guests in glistening mail
Laughed at the lady's whim.   The maid
Had only felt o'ercome, he said;
Perhaps, in bridal robes arrayed,
    She felt her courage fail.

VI.

"Albert," he cried, "go, seek thy bride!"
    And urged the noble youth,
Who quickly left the stately room
For lady's bower, although a gloom,
The mystic work of fancy's loom,
    O'erspread his thoughts in sooth.

VII.

'T was strange to grieve on bridal eve,
    When not a shade should rise
To dim his joyous dreams, but still
He felt a strange and piercing chill
Run through his gallant breast, until
    He paused in mute surprise.

VIII.

Beyond the stair, an alcove fair
    Was lighted from a sconce;
And, near the window, Lady Grace,
With blushes on her lovely face,
Addressed a youth of noble race,
    Who knelt there for the nonce.

53

IX.

With nodding crest, in leathern vest
    And chain-mail armor clad,
The handsome knight besought the bride
To leave her home, with all beside,
And venture o'er the distant tide.
    She whispered chidings sad :

X.

" For weal or woe, an hour ago,
    My troth I gave another;
Hadst thou but come yestreen, I might
Have happy been, but now, this night,
It is too late : haste, take to flight !
    I dare not grieve my mother;

XI.

"I should not pause, she'll learn the cause
 Of my strange absence; fly!
E'en while I live, I'll ne'er forget
Our youthful love; ah, stay! but yet
I should forget that we have met:
 Farewell, till worlds on high!—"

XII.

At Albert's tread, her visions fled;
 "Stay, villain!" fierce he breathed.
The lady shrieks, a strife begins;
Alas for her! whoever wins!
The cry, the clash of arms, soon thins
 The hall so gaily wreathed.

XIII.

From festive din the guests rush in ;
   The stranger knight is seized ;
But, ere that moment, on the floor
Young Albert lies in purple gore,
That proves the sword has pierced him sore,
   His wrath all unappeased.

XIV.

The baron orders faithful thralls
   To bear the caitiff knight
To some low dungeon, fettered well ;
But, ere they lead him to the cell,
The daring stranger shouts to tell
   His men-at-arms to fight.

XV.

The moonbeams gleam on many a pine,
    That shades the terrace high;
They glitter now on shining mail
Of comrade warriors: "Haste, assail,"
They answering cry, "the outer pale!
    The castle's weakness try!"

XVI.

With war's alarms, the men-at-arms
    Attack the barbacan:
The baron heads the garrison;
With shout and groan the fight rolls on:
The half-defended wall is won,
    By many a gallant man.

LADY GRACE'S BRIDAL.

XVII.

But, each that dares the massive stairs,
    A certain death awaits:
The grim old baron loves a fray;
Like sweep of avalanche his way,
When yonder foemen first essay
    To seize the inner gates.

XVIII.

Through combats fierce they onward pierce,
    Outnumbered, then retire;
When darksome mists the archway shroud,
They pause; and soon a murky cloud
Of vapor warns the baron proud
    His castle is on fire!

58

XIX.

For haughtiest mien an awful scene!
　The fire spreads the while:
Its dangers calm the baron's pride;
For Lady Grace, the lovely bride,
Still prays in grief by Albert's side,
　Within the ancient pile.

XX.

A prize untold of treasured gold
　He'll give to save her now;
A score, at least, the venture try;
'T is useless.　Must that fair one die
'Mid flames and smoke?　A sudden cry
　Of "Rescue!" smooths his brow.

59

LADY GRACE'S BRIDAL.

XXI.

The knotted rope now proffers hope,
    For, slowly down its strands,
The hardy knight with ease descends;
While all his utmost care he lends
To guard the lovely bride, he tends,
    From danger, ere she lands.

XXII.

The tower's base reach friends apace,
    And soon the pallid bride,
In terror, seeks her father's arms;
But, while he soothes her wild alarms,
He asks for Albert, while she charms
    With tears his haughty pride.

XXIII.

"Close to my side young Albert died!"
    She sobbed in accents low:
"I would not leave him, but he's dead;
His blood is on my guilty head;
A cloistered life must now be led
    By her who caused this woe!"

XXIV.

Soft peal the bells o'er lonely cells
    In yonder abbey gray:
This morn a maid, of beauty rare,
Has left the world with all its care,
If matin chimes and cloister air
    May soothe her griefs away.

XXV.

A saintly face had Lady Grace;
 And when she died, 't is said,
A wreath of roses was each day,
By stranger hands, placed o'er her clay:
The nuns at vespers ever pray
 Their lives like hers be sped.

THE STORM KING.

I.

The Storm King rose from his northern lair,
Shaking the rime from his frosty hair;
In wrath he cried: "To the South I'll go,
And shroud the world in a robe of snow!"

II.

His misty form, like an iceberg's shaft,
Gleams o'er the drifting, glacial raft,
While Northern Lights flame round his eyes,
And whirlwinds at his tread arise!

III.

The North Wind roared in his Arctic home:
"I'll follow thee, monarch, across the foam,
Where many a laden argosy
Will rue the hour it met with me!"

IV.

The Storm King spread his pinions wide,
And bore the North Wind at his side:
The forests groaned as the gale flew by,
Sweeping the branches toward the sky!

V.

The rivers foamed with a maddening glee,
And shoreward dashed a stormy sea,
Lashing the beach and the rocky strand,
Surging to whelm the hated land!

THE STORM KING.

VI.

Billow on billow mounts on high,
Till foaming crests to bubbles fly;
Wildly they struggle, with angry roar:
"T' is useless strife with the rugged shore!

VII.

The Storm King cried: "I'll onward sweep
O'er yonder wide and sullen deep;
My lordly sway has taught the wave,
In stormy winds, to foam and rave!"

VIII.

The North Wind blew o'er a noble fleet,
As it lay at rest, on the glassy sheet
Of a sheltered haven: "Come," he cried,
"I'll prove yon ships against the tide!"

IX.

Sudden and sharp was his icy breath ;—
The mariners sleep the sleep of death ;
The gallant fleet, that morn so gay,
Has foundered in the treacherous bay !

X.

Onward the terrible pair proceed ;
They deem yon wreck a glorious deed ;
And now, with a storm of heaviest rain,
They dash o'er the dark and troubled main !

XI.

The thunder peals o'er the vasty deep,
Aroused from its transient, quiet sleep ;
And lightning's flash shows many a bark
Laboring hard in the tempest dark !

THE STORM KING.

XII.

The ocean roars in the mighty blast,
As the mariner clings to his tottering mast;
But morning's sun will show the sea
Alone in its immensity!

XIII.

Across the foam the Storm King blows
A blast that tells of the northern snows;
And, driving the tide with a mighty roar,
They sweep in wrath to the distant shore!

XIV.

The North Wind breathed o'er the banks of cloud,
And chilled the drops that his pinions ploughed;
The sparkling flakes and rattling hail
Increase the awe of the rising gale!

THE STORM KING.

XV.

With roar and crash the North Wind flies;
The Storm King looks with wrathful eyes;
And, when his slave has wreaked his worst,
He joins the turmoil as at first!

XVI.

The storm will leave poor wives to weep
The loss of their all on the briny deep;
While young and old, of every age,
Will mourn, in vain, the tempest's rage!

XVII.

Howe'er proud man may spread his sway,
The Storm King rules the winds to-day,
As when, at Creation's dawn, he rose
To war with the sea and land, his foes!

IDYLS OF NIAGARA.

THE CAVE OF THE WINDS.

I.

As my footstep gains yon portal, swells within me the immortal!
  Earth's glories pale, Niagara! when we would thread thy foam:
Surging down with roar and quiver, comes the awful, thundering river,
  As through the veil of spray we glide, and tread the Wind King's dome.

II.

With a hush of expectation, in a glow of contemplation,
  Enwrapped in foaming, stormy mists, we reach the cliff beyond;
While caverned rocks behind us would, with solemn groan, remind us
  We covenant with Danger, would we burst her iron bond.

69

III.

See a land of wonder open! as the charm of storm is broken,
　Where rainbows gleam in beauty, deep in Nature's mystic shrine;
While the circling tints, uniting, paint Apocalyptic writing,
　Till bright-winged seraphs greet us in a presence so divine!

IV.

For rapt, entranced, with gazing at the sunlight brightly blazing
　On the awful, shadowy whiteness of the grand, majestic fall;
On radiant wings victorious, float the visions ever glorious,
　Till shines the great, white throne of Him who reigns in starry hall!

V.

While the emerald rainbow gleaming, as it quivers in its beaming,
　Circles round yon snowy emblem of the throne in Patmos seen,
Till the elders' voices reach us, and their holy accents teach us
　To cast our crowns before the throne, with faith's adoring mien!

IDYLS OF NIAGARA.

A VIEW FROM THE "MAID OF THE MIST."

I.

Beneath an arch of gleaming tints that spans a rushing tide,
Our struggling bark draws near a scene of whirlpools eddying wide ;
Where roaring waters foaming meet, that late, an emerald surge,
Swept grandly in a storm-girt flood, o'er yonder time-worn verge.

II.

The sunbeams glow, where, 'mid the spray, the hastening rapids dash ;
While winds in torment raving sweep, with more than Furies' lash ;
The fatal Maelström never raged with such stupendous might,
As where the gale-swept, whirling foam brings Chaos back, and Night !

71

IDYLS OF NIAGARA.

III.

The fall, where circling rainbows meet, sends up a mighty sound;
While yonder glorious Horseshoe curve of waters shakes the ground:
But, floating on a stormy wave between their thunder-peals,
The cresting, deep, eternal surge its grandest power reveals.

IV.

Commingling seas hurl cataracts, that claim a blended name,
Transcending all the falls on earth, in grandeur as in fame:
The ocean seems to crest a verge, supreme in curving sweep,
Whose thunders share the majesty that crowns the conquering deep!

V.

From altar-cliffs, the mist, like smoke of sacrifice and prayer,
Wafts up, as Nature's pæan wakes the floods and ambient air;
The tinted bow of promise floats on wings of cloudy spray,
And wondrous anthems seem to bring the Heavens near to-day!

IDYLS OF NIAGARA.

THE LUNAR RAINBOW.

I.

The dreamy moonlight lingers on Niagara's pale sheen;
While strange, fantastic shadows troop, the flood-worn cliffs between,
Where, weirdly rising through the spray, a fairy arch of light,
With ghostly gleams of color, springs,—a vision wondrous bright!

II.

A bow of purest silver, tinged with iridescent dyes,
Or like the magic scimitar a paladin would prize,
It gleams as though 't were brandished, by the startled Queen of Night,
To dare the rushing cataract, while foaming in its might!

73

IDYLS OF NIAGARA.

III.

The spray mounts up to waft it in a leap from shore to shore,
While, through the shadowy portal, comes a diapason roar,
Majestical in cadence, too sublime for mortal speech,
That breathes the mighty mystery these awful surges teach!

IV.

It thrills in mournful music to the soul that listens well:
"For ever, and for ever!" seems from out the surge to swell,
As yon abyss of tempest-mist receives the thundering wave,
While, o'er the river, stormy gusts amid the foam-clouds rave!

V.

The phantoms' hour of night draws near: the Storm King mounts on high:
And slowly fades the moonlight from the dark, tempestuous sky:
The mystic arch is gone, and hark! the river's thunder tone
Invokes the lightnings, till they vie in grandeurs of their own!

THE CLOCK TOWER, VENICE,

IN 1856.

———

Ye Giants, ever thundering forth the hour with measured clang!
How proudly once your answering strokes through yon piazza rang,
When dark, mysterious Venice hushed her citizens to sleep,
And bade them rest, for chosen ones the Doge's watch would keep!
The moonlight played o'er broad canals, reflecting lofty towers,
Where nobles revelled joyously through midnight's darkest hours:
What recked they if a comrade's face were blotted out from men?
The dark canal received the fool that braved the noble Ten!
Yet strike, ye brazen Giants! though the Doge's sway be past,
And Austrian standards wave, alas! from each imperial mast.
Ye call up dreams of olden times, while figures, strange and quaint,
Move by, as yonder puppets bow before their carven saint.
I see the ancient city when she ruled the open seas!
But though her flag brought wealth where'er it met the genial breeze,

THE CLOCK TOWER, VENICE.

And Venice glowed in splendor, yet her empire o'er the sea
Was not enjoyed by citizens that loved true liberty.
Ye shades of ancient heroes who adorned this mighty town!
Come back to earth, and tell us,—though your lives ye oft laid down
When Venice bade ye battle,—did not Carthaginian pride
Reign fiercely in the bosom of the Adriatic's bride?
It is a jealous sway when men refrain from honest speech:
It was not freedom when the sword hung o'er the head of each:
The proud Venetians kissed the rod, and deemed such rule the best,
But liberty they scarcely knew, or never deigned to test.
Ring out, thou clanging bell, aye, peal! but ring for better days,
When Venice, taught by tyranny, may sound true freedom's praise!

St. Mark's is glowing in the calm and pallid, silvery light,
Thrown wide in sparkling torrents from the radiant orb of night:
An Eastern tale in marble is that hoary, ancient pile,
Where Barbarossa bowed his neck, o'ercome by papal wile.
A shadowy, gay procession sweeps along the open square,—
The Emperor comes to Venice, with a penitential air;
That mighty Barbarossa fears yon priest's bejewelled cope,

THE CLOCK TOWER, VENICE.

And must atone for injuries to Rome's imperious Pope;
The Empire kneels before the Church, and Alexander dares
To place his foot upon the neck of one of Cæsar's heirs!
The shadows fade, while o'er the bay come morning's earliest beams,
But daylight, here in Venice, cannot break the spell of dreams;
A long day-dream it is to roam through mouldering marble piles,
And hear the gondolier's slow plash awake the silent isles:
The dark canals, the lofty towers and temples, thickly strewn,
The dreams of wildest fantasy, slow mouldering in stone,
The stillness of the watery streets, scarce broken by a sound,
Impress the laden fancy so, its wings would touch the ground!

The Doge's Palace frowns beside St. Mark's majestic throne,—
Yet doges were oft shadows, while as phantoms they have flown:
The Giants' Staircase, and the spot where Faliero's head
Rolled down the marble steps, to join the armies of the dead,
May draw a tear or passing sigh, at least the solemn thought,
That vengeance, such as that he sought, were far too dearly bought!
St. Mark's winged lion still looks down from yonder column's height,
A token of the proud Republic's ancient strength and might;

THE CLOCK TOWER, VENICE.

The Gaul restored his trophy, conquered Paris missed it not,
While Venice feels that lion's sway can never be forgot!

O golden, dreamy Venice! who would roam the world alone,
When old, historic friends seem beckoning from each sculptured stone!
The world drifts madly by thee, yet it cannot mar thy peace;
While centuries roll back their gates, all cares and troubles cease.
Mysterious City! when we gaze on pinnacle and dome,
And see thee rise, like Venus fair, from out the sparkling foam,
A dreamy wonder fills the soul, and, floating o'er the waves,
Thy distant chimes seem fairies' song, upborne from ocean caves!

AFTER THE WRECK.

I.

The whirlwind smote the gallant ship: she sank beneath the waves;
The ocean roared in angry tones around the sailors' graves!
A daring youth alone survived, to gain a dreary beach;
And thus lamented to the surge, as sorrow gave him speech:

II.

"Awake bright day! A lonely watch of agony I keep!
Wildly rave the billows: sadly moans the deep:
She, who slumbers by me on the dark and desert shore,
Sleeps too soundly, breakers, to be wakened by your roar!

III.

"Bright her golden ringlets glance in yonder dawning light;
But the pallid moon, that shone so weirdly in the night,
Kissed her cheeks so coldly, that their rosy color fled:
`Alice, wake! Ah, nothing wakes the slumbers of the dead!

79

AFTER THE WRECK.

IV.

"Seaweed garlands deck her curls, the work of ocean nymphs,
Wrought when, swept from floating masts, she vanished at a glimpse!
Coldly closed the waters round her fair, ethereal form,
Far too fragile e'er to live through such a raging storm!

V.

All are gone! and I, alas! survive the awful wreck!
Alice! little thought we, when we paced the quiet deck,
I should only, of our crew, in safety reach the land,
And hold my darling in these arms, alone upon the strand!

VI.

"Break, proud day! I care not for thy brightest, golden beams:
She is gone who ever reigned sole idol of my dreams!
Ocean, come! I hail thy waves! the tide, now rising high,
Will sweep me from the narrow strand;—near Alice I shall die!"

A PASTORAL.

Pleasant groves and laughing brooks !
Aye, ye cool and shady nooks,
Where the trout, in countless numbers,
Wake the waters from their slumbers :
Ye, I hail, when summer's sun
Hath its burning heat begun :
When the branches, drooping, quiver
O'er the cool, refreshing river ;
And the songster's merry trill
Echoes from the silent mill,
Where, upon the moss-grown wheel,
Many happy pairs conceal
Glossy eggs from curious eyes,
Lest some boy may make a prize
Of the nest so neatly twined,
Which their careful beaks have lined

81

A PASTORAL.

With the softest hair and down :
Shame, that any country clown
Should be found to spoil the labor
Of his pretty, feathered neighbor!

See! the stream, that once of old
Turned the mill that brought the gold
To the rich, old miller's purse,—
Where it proved a speedy curse,—
Now, released from wooden gloom,
Foams above the moss-grown flume :
Blithely leaps adown the vale,
Pausing here to fill a pail,
Left by careful lass to cool
In the deepest of the pool ;
Hurrying now adown a steep,
With a playful, merry leap ;
Here, entangled in the willows,
Foaming apes the ocean's billows.

A PASTORAL.

Merry brook ! I love its glee,
As it sparkles merrily
In the sunbeam's scattered light,—
Where it threads the leafy night,—
Hailing here the golden day,
As through meadows ripe for hay,
Bursting from the shady grove,
Where it loved so long to rove ;
Laughing at the waving grass,
That will hardly let it pass
Ere it slyly steals a kiss,—
On it hastes to yon abyss ;
Boldly plunging down the height,
With a wanton, gay delight ;
Hiding with a silvery veil,
Shaken by the passing gale.
Every rugged, rocky feature,
Like a merry, laughing creature !

A PASTORAL.

Lovely vales! that far below
Sparkle in the sunlight's glow,
Greet this merry brook for me,
As it hastens to the sea :
Fold your tender arms around it :
Keep it spotless as ye found it !
In yon dark and rapid river,
All that sparkle, all that quiver,
Will be lost amid the tide,
As it chafes the vessel's side.
Restless brook ! thy playful stream
Tells the whole of life's long dream,
As thou prattlest to the herds
All the love-songs of the birds ;
How they sang about the Spring,
Or swept round on rapid wing,
Skimming o'er thy brimming fount,
On the distant, verdant mount.
Now, a deep and crystal wave,
Thou canst roll along the nave

A PASTORAL.

Formed by arching trees above,
Where the birds still whisper love :
But thy ripples, as they foam,
Sigh for that sweet, mountain home.

LADY BELLE.

Loud yelled the castle-hounds at morn, in early, warm September;
   The drawbridge fell, and Lady Belle right gallantly rode out.
That morning, all the hamlet folk,—who pitied her,—remember,
   Recalling well her winning smile and pretty, dimpling pout.
That stern Lord William's temper could not change, although he vainly
   Essayed to bend the wilful girl, who mocked his angry mien:
Lord William she ne'er loved, nay, called him ugly and ungainly,
   And all declared he suited not her beauty, that a queen
Might envy. She was lovely! fair as early, blushing summer,
   When roses shed a fragrant gale of perfume on the air:
Lord William, if at Christmas-tide he figured as a mummer,
   Would make the saddest mourner laugh, the sleepiest baron stare.
Forth rode the lovely lady, in the dew of early morning,
   To hunt the stag; she turned her steed towards a distant glade:
The branches stooped to greet her, as the pallid light, then dawning,
   Shone weirdly on her beauty, till each early village maid,

LADY BELLE.

Who met her, almost shuddered as she courtesied to the lady,
    Whose alms outvied her beauty,—for she was a bounteous dame;
Aye, many an eye looked after, as the forest deep and shady
    Received the lovely woman, fully worthy of her name.
Lady Belle, return! Lord William, though you thought he slumbered soundly,
    Heard every voice this morning, as in yonder tower he lay:
O, venture not too rashly! for he storms and curses roundly,
    And calls thee, gentle lady, all too wild, and far too gay.
From yonder lofty turret he has watched thy groom's devotion,
    While by a secret postern-gate he leaves the castle now;
A courser there awaits him, he will mount without commotion,
    And follow every foot-print, with a shadow on his brow.
Beware, thou gentle lady! Rumor says—and some believe it—
    Yon handsome groom is gentle, and no stable-youth by birth:
Lord William dreams he's Edgar, thy old love; then wherefore leave it
    To Scandal's tongue, fair lady, to proclaim it o'er the earth?
Why must that groom be ever at thy bridle-rein when riding?
    Dismiss him, gentle lady! 't is a trial to be borne;
Though he tells sweet, forest legends, yet allow no room for chiding:
    'T were well he left thy palfrey's side, if only on this morn.

LADY BELLE.

Nay, Lady Belle is wilful, and she loves to hear traditions
    Related by the handsome groom, that holds her bridle-rein ;
But, while she stoops intently, all Lord William's dull suspicions
    Are fanned to flame ; he rides in jealous fury o'er the plain.
Low howled the hounds at midnight, as a single cry of terror
    Disturbed the placid stillness of the calm September night ;
A spotless lady, falsely charged by jealousy with error,
    Lies bleeding on the chapel floor, a woful, piteous sight !
The cross she clasps is reddened with her life-blood's crimson blushes,
    And deep her ermine robe is stained with that untimely dye :
Her maidens found the corse, at early morn, among the rushes,
    Where painted windows rain soft rays the secret to descry.

THE WATER FAY.

Far in a cool and darksome pool,
  Of a quiet, mountain glen,
A water fay contented lay,
  In a cataract's spray : but when
The rainbow gleamed on the waterfall,
  With its tinted arch of light,
And beamed on the heavy, mossy pall
  That hid the spring from sight,
The fay grew weary of the gloom,
  And longed to see the day,
To view the sun, whose radiant loom
  Could weave such colors gay.
She asked the breeze and the sparkling spray,
  What was there 'yond the vale,
To which the gladsome orb of day
  Followed the eastern gale.

THE WATER FAY.

The merry breeze, with a playful shake,
    Removed the mossy pall,
And showed, beside a distant lake,
    A castle vast and tall:
"I often blow by the western tower,
    And see a youthful knight
Look out and greet the sunset hour,
    Or morning's golden light.
For years I've watched his slender form
    Expand to manhood's mien:
I fan his brow, and in the storm
    Oft kiss his cheek, unseen."

The fay, enraptured, lists too well,
    For, when the breeze is gone,
She fain would break the slender spell,
    That binds her, every morn,
To sink beneath the bubbling spring,
    And bring a jewel up,

THE WATER FAY.

To grace her queen, as a beauteous ring,
　　Or deck her golden cup.
She longs to view the distant tower
　　Where dwells the youthful knight.
And wearies of her mossy bower,
　　To which the golden light
Of early day can hardly reach.
　　To tinge the quiet pool.
The breeze has told of a pebbly beach.
　　With grottoes deep and cool.
Where many a sister fay is seen
　　Amid the laughing waves:
Where Undines, clothed in seaweed green,
　　Command obedient slaves
To bring them pearls from the briny sea
　　To deck their waving hair;
And play in merry, sportive glee,
　　Without a thought of care:
"Oh would I were a fair Undine.
　　And free to leave my spring.

THE WATER FAY.

To deck my hair with the jewels rare
    From the watery depths I would bring!"

The cataract breathed in her listening ear:
    "Sweet fay, but follow me,
I'll bear thee away, in my torrent's play,
    To the distant, deep, blue sea:
We'll plunge o'er the dark and frowning rock
    To the lovely vale below;
A fay can bear the sudden shock,
    Enwrapped in my silvery flow."
"Farewell for aye, my native grot!"
    The fairy whispered low:
"Farewell! in future I shall not
    Know fear of ice or snow.
My bubbling spring, for aye adieu!
    Thy cool and pleasant well
Must fade, forever, from my view;
    Fair, jewelled depths, farewell!"

THE WATER FAY.

The torrent twined its misty arms
   Around the timid fay:
She feels her grot has many charms,
   As now she glides away;
Yet how endure her haughty queen,
   Whose brilliant diadem
Claims, for its now unrivalled sheen,
   Each new-discovered gem!
She fancies, then, the ocean sprites,
   And that fair, sparkling lake.
Where she will rest for many nights,
   And see the water-snake
Erect its glossy head on high
   Above the waters blue:
She views the open, sunny sky.
   And feels the breeze said true.

Enwrapped in a misty veil of spray.
   They leap the lofty height.

THE WATER FAY.

And float away with the torrent's play
　　In the rainbow's varied light.
Through many a green and flowery mead,
　　The river pours along:
The frightened fay can hardly heed
　　The bird's melodious song;
Her sister sprites come flocking near
　　To see the stranger fay,
And wonder from what distant mere
　　She can have swum away;
They offer water-lilies bright,
　　And gems of varied hue,
But, till the fall be lost to sight,
　　The fay must speed anew;
She dreads her queen's imperious wrath,
　　And fears the tattling breeze
May point her wild and dangerous path,
　　Ere she has reached the seas.
Amid the fairies of the lake
　　She hopes for safety soon;

THE WATER FAY.

Already she can see them shake
  Their locks, as the rising moon
With mellow radiance softly shines
  On the castle, grim and old,
Enwrapped in countless, wanton vines,
  That veil its outlines bold.

'T were a merry sight to watch the fays,
  As lovingly they play;
No mortal eye can ever gaze
  On revels half so gay:
They chase the pretty, sportive fish,
  Who know no thought of fright,
For fairies in their pastimes wish
  The finny tribe no spite.
They gather merrily to hail
  Their new companion now,
Recall the rose to features pale,
  And kiss her weary brow.

THE WATER FAY.

Anon they lead her to a bower,
    Beneath the waters blue.
Adorned with many a water-flower,
    And radiant to the view.—
With water-lilies crowned, their queen
    Receives the timid sprite,
Arrayed in robes of deep sea-green,
    All sparkling in the light
That filters through the watery dome
    In bright, yet softened, rays:
She bids the fairy welcome home,
    And kindly then displays
The thousand treasures of the waves,
    The heaps of gems untold,
And pearls, for which a fairy braves
    The ocean deep and cold.

"O joyous life," the fay exclaimed,
    "To live beneath the sea.

THE WATER FAY.

And view the secrets, all unnamed,
  Of ocean's majesty ;
To sport amid the gay Undines,
  And through the coral caves ;
To gaze on new and varied scenes
  Beneath the stormy waves!"
"O fay, beware!" the monarch cries,
  " We fairies of the lake,
Who scent the salt breeze as it flies,
  Can hardly undertake
The journey to the deep sea grots,
  Where dwell the ocean fays :
The demons weave their wicked plots
  To tempt the unwary gaze ;
They pile up lofty coral reefs
  To check our toilsome course,
And, led by bold and daring chiefs,
  Use every known resource
To check our progress : yes, they dare
  To bring the cuttle-fish,

THE WATER FAY.

And darken every wave, nor spare
    The Undines, if they wish
To guide us through the watery night.
    Then fay, beware the sea!
But wherefore roam? Nay, stay thy flight!
    And live in peace with me;
I'll guard thee from thy haughty queen,
    She dares not venture here;
I care not for her angry mien,
    For she has learned to fear
The gentle fairies of the lake,
    When roused by proud disdain:
Then here thy home in future make,
    Nor seek the angry main."

The fay is but too happy, now,
    To bend the humble knee,
And vow allegiance, with a brow
    From every trouble free.

THE WATER FAY.

Now, o'er the sparkling silver sheet,
  She sports in frolic wild ;
The breeze comes laughing her to greet,
  Yet breathes, in accents mild :
" Alas, thy lone, deserted well !
  The water sighs for thee ;
I hardly blow o'er the leafy dell,
  Its charms are gone for me.
Yet here the castle frowns above ;
  And see ! the youthful knight
Looks out, and dreams of aught but love :
  His pleasure is the fight !
O, win him to the quiet lake,
  By many a ripple's play !
He often will a ramble take
  To watch the fading day."

A silvery shower of rippling pearls
  The fairy throws on high,

THE WATER FAY.

Anon, a misty wave she hurls
 Towards the evening sky ;
The moonbeams softly play around
 The gently scattering spray,
While, hear that wild melodious sound !
 The love-song of the fay :
" O, wander to the pebbly beach,
 Thou gentle cavalier !
And let my loving accents reach
 Thy kind, attentive ear :
I'll bring thee pearls and perfumed flowers,
 The water-lilies rare
I'll gather in our island bowers,
 To deck thy raven hair."
" I hear the whispering of the breeze,"
 The warrior, wondering, says,
" How sweet it murmurs through the trees,
 Like some forgotten lays.
The moon is bright, my skiff I'll take,
 And row a pleasant mile ;

THE WATER FAY.

I have not crossed yon silvery lake
   This many a weary while."
He leaves the shore, and guides his bark
   Towards a distant beach :
Farewell, thou wanderer of the dark,
   That shore thou'lt never reach !
By elfin arms, his slender skiff
   Is dragged beneath the wave :
A stone upon a neighboring cliff
   Records his watery grave.
From earth he's gone, but, 'neath the lake,
   In long, enchanted sleep,
The fairies all their play forsake,
   A guard o'er him to keep :
The fay entwines her glistening arms
   Around his slumbering form,
And keeps him, by her magic charms,
   From tempest and from storm.

THE EXILE.

O mournful, sighing, stormy wind, blow far my grief from me!
And let me gentle solace find, beside the moaning sea :
In mighty chords, the ocean swells a harmony sublime,
That thrills like chime of Sabbath bells, in our fair, distant clime :
In plaintive cadence come the sounds, as though the village spire
Soared heavenward beyond these mounds, that gleam in sunset's fire!

The sea, that thunders on the shore it lashes with its spray,
Still bears our country's navies, o'er the waves they proudly sway!—
When heroes struck for Freedom's right, a gallant warrior band,
Then tyranny revealed its might, and drove us from the land !
The flag we honored with our blood salutes the breeze to-day,
As when we bore it o'er this flood, a tyrant's power to stay!

THE EXILE.

'Mid roar of battle's answering guns, we waved that flag on high
Where valor bade earth's noblest sons, in glory's ranks, to die!
O Freedom! spread thy wings, again, across the glorious land
I hail, from o'er the sounding main that sweeps its rocky strand!

I walk o'erwhelmed with patriot woe! and what can comfort bring?
In vain, through joyous throngs I go, that float on Pleasure's wing:
The noble land I proudly claim has brighter charms divine
Than youth's enchanting dreams of fame with fairest hopes entwine.
The whisper of the murmuring brook once filled my soul with joy,
When, stretched in some familiar nook, I dreamed, a happy boy!
But now, I seek a grander scene, and hail the rolling sea;
Although, alas! it sighs between my native land and me!

OUR CAPTAIN'S ORDERS.

— ---

I.

Soldiers!—The trumpet sounds your orders:
　To skirmish, prompt, each man prepare!
Right shoulder shift!—See those maranders,
　That reconnoitre everywhere!

II.

In groups of four, brave comrades, keep united:
　Watch well, for horsemen hover round!
Pick off each man, till foes retreat affrighted:
　If on they charge, stand, stand your ground!

III.

Now, double quick; apart by twenty paces,
  March on and gain yon vantage height!
Then halt and fire! They come with eager faces:
  But, vanquished, soon will take to flight.

IV.

They gather fast, like clouds before the shower:
  Assemble, quick, on strong reserve!
The trumpet sounds, for dangers round us lower;
  They charge! Retreat! Strain every nerve!

V.

The ranks part wide; rush in and take your stations!
  On, on they come; now fire again!
Huzza, brave boys! Aye, give them powder rations!
  They break! They fly! We've cleared the plain!

BUONAROTTI'S DOME.

How light the imperious arches spring along the mighty nave,
To where the lamps their lustre fling above St. Peter's grave!
Encrusted marbles lead the gaze from point to point to roam,
Till mute we stand, in new amaze, beneath the awful dome:
The soul that dreamed this arching grand, to rear that dome on high,
Should ne'er have sought its native land, but soared to yonder sky!—
Now pace the aisles, while sunset flings its fading, mellow light,
In scattering gold-dust, on the wings of doves and cherubs bright:
Then view the ceiling, fretted o'er with massy weight of gold:
Or trace upon the marble floor the record there enrolled,
That tells the stretch of kindred piles, all dwindling into naught
Compared with these majestic aisles,—grand avenues of thought!
O Buonarotti! such as thou were born to show the world
The stamp of God upon our brow: and breathe the might, that hurled
Yon sun and planets to their place, and reared the cloudy dome,
By which thou—Titan of our race!—didst shape thy work at Rome.

MIRRORED CLOUDS.

I.

Far down in crystal caverns dwell the sprites that rule the river,
But, on a summer day, when all is peaceful, calm and still,
I trace their fairy structures, strange and weird, misshapen ever,
Lying far beneath the shadows of the trees on yonder hill.

II.

Like stalactites drooping downward from some cavern roof, they glimmer
In the scarcely noticed ripple of the calm, transparent stream ;
Ever changing with the clouds, the elfin edifices shimmer
Like strange, fantastic castles seen in some mysterious dream.

107

MIRRORED CLOUDS.

III.

Calmly floats the crystal river o'er the phantom, fairy towers,
   They vanish if we venture with too curious eyes to gaze;
Looming up anon they glitter, as the sun plays o'er the flowers,
   And elves come forth to frolic in the golden, misty haze.

IV.

Dreamy turrets, could we fathom to your magic caves of wonder,
   What treasures would we not espy within their crystal halls!
But elves allow the world to see but clouds reflected under,
   And watery depths allow us not to venture to your walls.

THE CORONATION OF THE CZAR.

MOSCOW, SEPT. 7, 1856.

———

I.

The Kremlin Towers, like Eastern Kings, arise,
   Where holy chapels greet the pilgrim's gaze;
As, from the sacred gate, with raptured eyes,
   He views the lofty domes in wondrous maze!
Ivan's proud tower rules the imperial halls:
While Michael's shrine the ancient Czars recalls;
For many an early Emperor lies there:—
Though Peter's City guards his dust with care.

THE CORONATION OF THE CZAR.

II.

The noble court-yard, where the staircase ends,
　By which processions rise to grand saloons,
Is filled with troops:—for war its tribute lends
　To grace the Czar, the source of glory's boons:—
A gay assemblage meets in colonnades,
All recent reared for guests of honored grades:
To-day the Czar assumes his father's crown;
And brightest skies of peace look smiling down.

III.

Colossus of the Eastern world of dreams,
　Majestic Russia! hail thy Czar to-day!
While countless millions praise the golden beams
　Of joyous peace, that bless this proud array:
Like Memnon, seated by Egyptian Nile,
And waked to music by the sun-god's smile,
The glowing rays from happier lands than thine
Attune thy might to harmony divine!

THE CORONATION OF THE CZAR.

IV.

Between the serried ranks, a crimson sweep
  Of avenues, prepared for stately show,
Glistens with copes and uniforms, as deep
  As when parterres' gay blossoms waving blow;
The clergy gather round yon chapel's gate,
With incense, banners bright, and robes of state:
From Ivan's reign, the Czars are ever crowned
Within this shrine, that gilded saints surround.

V.

A pontiff soon descends the palace-stair,
  While long-haired priests a glittering vessel raise;
The holy water, see! he scatters, where,
  To bless the Czar's advance, he humbly prays:
His vestments' glow attests his priestly might;
While soon he joins that group, in mitres bright,
Where Persian carpets veil the crimson floor,
And prelates, robed in gold, surround the door.

111

THE CORONATION OF THE CZAR.

VI.

There Philarete, the aged bishop, stands,
   To meet the Czar, and tender him the crown:
The populace would rush to kiss his hands,
   Could they but reach where guards on entrance frown:
Fair Moscow owns his gentle sway with pride;
The Russian church reveres in him a guide;
He now awaits the widowed Empress, here,
Who mourned so late beside a monarch's bier.

VII.

'Mid pealing chimes, a bright procession comes,
   The Empress Mother, canopied in state,
With diamonds ablaze, of royal sums,
   In cloth of gold and crown of costly weight:
A long array of nobles throngs the way,
And princesses with trains of colors gay :
The Czar's young heir beside the Empress goes,
Where tissue, borne on rods of silver, glows.

112

THE CORONATION OF THE CZAR.

VIII.

The jewelled cross, that Philarete extends,
   Is kissed in peace, and then the mitred throng
Escort the Empress, who her throne ascends
   Within the stately chapel's shrine of song:
Anon, the lordly prelates, at the gate,
In silent pause the Czar's advance await;
While officers remain a brilliant frame
Around the arms the sunlight tips with flame.

IX.

What scenes of horror once deformed this place,
   When haughty Bonaparte his legions led
To seize the royal shrine of Russia's race,—
   These towers,—that seemed as silent as the dead!
Then, patriot fires illumed each palace lone,
And flames rolled round the Kremlin's sacred zone;
Till mighty France, in terror, fled a land
That hurled new woes with such relentless hand.—

X.

A roar of cannon, with the clang of bells,
　Inform the world the Autocrat draws nigh,
While, louder yet, the joyful pæan swells
　As though to reach the smiling, distant sky:
Another pageant sweeps adown the stair,
Displaying gems that Russians only wear;
The courtiers pass in pairs, an endless train,
To grace, in state, their master's opening reign.

XI.

The ladies, robed in emerald velvet, come,
　Embroidered gay, adorned with golden moon
And floating veil; while, near their joyous hum,
　Pass princesses, like clouds before the noon:
A lordly train, with canopy of gold
Upheld by generals, comes, its wealth untold;
The Czar, in uniform of state, uncrowned;
The Empress, robed in white that sweeps the ground.

THE CORONATION OF THE CZAR.

XII.

Such pageantry, as gleams before our eyes,
    Shines with a splendor scarcely known to man,
As when the Northern Lights illume the skies,
    And, streaming to the zenith, crown their span :
The Czar moves on, with princes at his side,
While nobles throng in undistinguished tide,
Like comet, trailing through the brilliant night
A wondrous train, surpassing starry light.

XIII.

The cross is kissed, and then the proud array
    Of prelate, Czar and prince, deserts the morn ;
While bells peal forth to tell the listening day,
    The Czar in state the gorgeous crown has worn :
At length, the Empress Mother, with her train,
Resplendent seeks the palace-stair again ;
The new-crowned pair the farther gates have passed,
To march, beyond the walls, where throngs are massed.

XIV.

Like some mirage, the traveller, on the plain
    Or sandy desert, sees majestic rise,
These towers and domes seem works of Fancy's reign;
    The bright assemblage waits with eager eyes,—
As when, in tropic lands of balmy clime,
Where waves of silver roll their crests sublime,
And royal-palms droop fronds of dreamy grace,
The birds salute the sun's returning face.

XV.

The Czar, in grand procession, by the gate
    Near yonder church, appears upon the scene;
The diamond crown he wears, of massy weight.—
    An azure blaze of flame,—exalts his mien :
He looks a monarch firm, of gentle sway,
Whose crown of gems eclipses sunlight's ray,
Till, orb and sceptre, jewelled robes of gold
With ermine decked, the gaze can hardly hold !

THE CORONATION OF THE CZAR.

XVI.

The Empress fair, adorned with lesser crown,—
  Like rainbows gleaming,—moves in stately guise,
A golden mantle o'er her silken gown,
  While kindness beams within her lovely eyes:
The Czar uncrowns his head, then goes to pray,
Within St. Michael's church, for grace to-day;
Returning, soon the diamond dome he wears,
Which has no power to soothe a monarch's cares.

XVII.

Like Fortunatus, endless wealth is thine,
  Imperial Czar! Like river on its way,
That pours its stream 'mid hills that yield the vine,
  Refreshing thirsty fields through sunny day,
So flows thy kindness toward the suffering slave,
Till serfs, made free, shall all adore its wave.
Nations of every garb and tongue appear,
To hail their king, and bless the favored year!

117

XVIII.

The royal pageant wends its golden way,
  By yonder stair, all open to the skies,
To wondrous halls; magnificent display!
  There diamonds stud the doors,—a matchless prize,—
While malachite, in rich pilasters reared,
Delights as though some fairy-land appeared!
The Czar attends a feast with nobles proud,
Where custom's sway is reverently allowed.

XIX.

At night, all Moscow flames with joyous lights,
  The Kremlin towers are dazzling seas of fire,
While garden-trees, as in "Arabian Nights,"
  Seem decked with colored gems, in radiant pyre;
St. Basil's shrine, like fountain-jets of flame,
Beams fairer than when Ivan praised its fame,
And palaces, along the river, seem
To make this eve too bright for poet's dream.

LOOKOUT MOUNTAIN, TENNESSEE.

———

Look out o'er yonder valley fair where flows the Tennessee,
In bends unnumbered sweeping round to waters ever free;
There Chattanooga nestles by the turbid, rushing stream,
And Missionary Ridge up-springs,—a scene for patriot's dream!
The mist oft drifts where charmed we stand, and view a cloudless sky;
But war has raged amid the clouds in years now scarce flown by.
Then noble Grant his armies led from Chattanooga town,
And sent brave Hooker here to drive the fierce insurgents down;
For rebels held these very heights, those few, short years ago,
When Bragg essayed to keep our arms beyond that river's flow.
While Sherman stormed yon lofty ridge, bold Hooker led his men
Among the clouds, to fight the foe beside his mountain den:
Then, glory fired their dauntless hearts for Union's sake to die,
Or wrest from out the jaws of death the prize of victory!

119

LOOKOUT MOUNTAIN, TENNESSEE.

Rebellion fled before our arms; the heights were nobly won:
And from the clouds the stars and stripes were greeted by the sun.
The gateway to the South then ours by Grant and Sherman's arms,
Yon valley smiled on freedom soon, with all its peerless charms.
Then gaze on Lookout Mountain well, where shot and shell have played,
And bless the noble hearts that won the heights, all undismayed!

FAIRY TALES OF THE TROPICS.

The Elves are blithe, fantastic sprites,
　　And dwell in caverns fair,
Whose crystal frostwork e'er invites
　　The gaze with jewels rare;
Their Monarch reigns o'er wondrous isles
　　That deck the glowing deep
In tropic climes; for Nature smiles
　　Where elves her brilliants keep.
While thus the Elf King's regal sway
　　Extends o'er sunny lands,
The Gnomes a rival chief obey,
　　Where gleam the golden sands:
Their King reigns o'er a mighty isle,
　　Whose mines exalt his sway;
And deep, volcanic fire, the while,
　　He rules with fierce display.

A Fairy Queen's vast kingdom bright,
   Beneath more distant skies,
Adorns the island group of light
   Where towering mountains rise:
Her subjects wander through the isles
   To seek the jasmine flowers,
Whose perfume floats for balmy miles,
   And wreathe entrancing bowers.
The Elf King was for magic famed:
   Thus when enchanters came
To try their powers, his might proclaimed
   How he deserved his name:
His favorite Elf a wizard slew
   That strove to bind the King;
Who, for his loyal service true,
   Adorned each gleaming wing,
Then gave a mystic, jewelled sword
   To guard from every foe;
Its power had often saved its lord,
   Who charmed each deadly blow.

The Gnome King loved a beauteous Fay,
　　That would not heed his prayer,
And smiled to see him oft display
　　Rich gems and blossoms rare:
She was a lovely, bright-winged maid,
　　Who, with her sister, dwelt
Within a fairy grotto's shade,
　　Where oft her lover knelt.
Her jealous sister loved the Gnome,
　　And longed to win his heart;
But he preferred to fondly roam,
　　In hope, by some new art,
To woo the lovely, blue-eyed Fay
　　To be his queenly bride:
While oft, in knightly, rich array,
　　He sought her o'er the tide.
The Elf King ordered revels gay,
　　Within his magic grot,
And prayed each charming, island Fay
　　To seek the favorite spot.

The sisters twain resolved to go;
  And crossed the tranquil main
In pearly shells, illumed to glow
  Beneath each shining train.
The Gnome King warned them not to leave
  Their peaceful, island shade;
Then said a weird mischance would grieve
  Their hearts, without his aid:
He gave the Fay a jewel bright,
  And bade her prove its power
Whene'er its talismanic might
  Could save in danger's hour.
The sisters sought the cavern's light;
  And left the Royal Gnome
To guard their grot from ouphe and sprite,
  While they were o'er the foam:
They floated, as on wings of fate,
  While moonbeams filled the air,
To where the Elf King reigns in state
  Within his grotto fair!

THE ELVES' GROTTO.

———

In sparkling grots of wondrous hues,
   Beside the tropic sea,
The elves hold revels, and amuse
   The fairies with their glee :
Borne on the silvery waves, they come
   To join the elfin court ;
Then sounds a mystic, joyous hum
   Of wildest, fairy sport;
They climb the fragile pillars fair,
   Where flowers, they cull afar,
Are chained by magic powers of air,
   Each with a crystal star.

Amid these scenes of revelry,
   A Fairy, musing, gazed;—
While, moored beside the moonlit sea,
   Her pearly bark still grazed
The shining coral reef:—she dreamed
   Of many a distant shore,
Where grots of paler radiance beamed
   That charmed her fancy more;
Of lovely isles, whose beauteous palms
   More wondrous ever seemed,
When wandering 'mid the richer charms
   With which this magic gleamed:
"O joyous land of flowers!" she thought,
   "Where glows the Torrid sun,
And Nature yields her gifts, unsought,
   Why was my life begun!
I dwelt a happy fay till now,
   But, since the Gnome King's power
Has poured his gifts to deck my brow,
   I scarcely prize my bower;

THE ELVES' GROTTO.

My sister loved me well till then,
　But now she colder grows:
Ah, would I could live o'er again
　Those hours, ere youth shall close!"
Her sister watched her dreamy mood,
　And sighed: "Ah, happy maid!
Thou dreamest of the Gnome that wooed
　Fair charms that soon will fade;
He cared not for my lustrous eyes,
　But prized thy orbs of blue;
Though storms between us twain arise,
　His faith shall not prove true:
I well deserve the jewelled crown,
　That should be mine by right;
The gallant Gnome shall cast it down
　Before my raptured sight;
And we shall reign amid the mines
　That glitter in our groves,
Where wreathe the wondrous, perfumed vines
　To tempt the ouphe that roves."

127

She viewed her sister's dreamy face,
   Which now more blushing grew:
The lovely Fay, with witching grace,
   Reclined, in musings new:
Till, waking now, she beaming smiled;
   For, darting through the fays,
A merry Elf her dreams beguiled
   With dance, to win her gaze;
Now, floated airily between
   The slender columns bright;
Then, hovering near, with joyous mien,
   Soft fanned her wings of light.
"Oh, prithee, come with me," he sang,
   "To our proud Monarch's throne;
And plight thy troth, where crystals hang
   In wondrous, mazy zone!"
"Nay!" softly breathed the dreamy Fay,
   "My home, beyond the sea,
Has sprites as fair, and hearts as gay,
   I may not list to thee."

128

THE ELVES' GROTTO.

The jealous sister murmured low:
  "This Elf, who loves her well,
May aid my purpose, that will show,
   Who best a Queen should dwell!"
She whispered to the joyous Elf:
  "Wouldst gain my sister's hand?
A lover bold then prove thyself:—
   She should not quit this land:—
A wondrous jewel decks her hair,
   That can her freedom gain,
Yet 't will be used but in despair;
   With gnomes she will not reign.
Thy kindly Monarch will approve,
   Then seek his splendid throne,
And win her by a daring move,
   She will be thine alone!"—
The Elf drew near the dreaming Fay,
   And shook his wand of light;
The Fairy started, in dismay,
   To feel its potent might:

A rainbow chariot rose in pride,
  Her lover charmed the car
To waft the winning, captive bride
  To halls that beamed afar.
The filmy bats, he harnessed, bore
  The chariot on its way,
And many an elf flew on before,
  To lead to pageants gay;
The sister Fairy swiftly sped
  Beside their airy flight;
While, with the Fay, whose senses fled,
  Fast drove the elfin knight.

A throne was reared of dazzling gems;
  And crowned with glistening pearl,
His feet on priceless diadems,
  The Monarch watched the whirl
Of mazy dances, 'neath a dome
  With crystal glories bright,

THE ELVES' GROTTO.

Where sparkling gardens made their home
  In fairy bowers of light.
The chariot whirled before the throne,
  And soon the elfin youth
Implored, with many a tender moan,
  His Monarch's aid: " In sooth,
Great Sovereign!" he, appealing, cried,
  " But grant my humble prayer.
And bid this charming fairy guide
  My life, that we may share
The glories of thy mighty reign :
  Oh, bid her list to me,
And I will face the stormy main,
  Or brave the world for thee !"
The lovely Fay responded: " King!
  I crossed the silver deep
To view a grot the Muses sing.
  And joyous feast to keep.
Proud Monarch! break this fearful charm,
  And let me flee away:

Or thou shalt feel the Gnome King's arm
    Before the break of day !"
The Monarch gazed, in kindly mood,
    And wondered at the scene ;
But pity, for an elf that wooed
    A fay of coldest mien,
With royal justice struggled well :
    And courtiers gathered near,
To hear his lips the verdict tell
    And Fay or lover cheer.
At length the Elf King muttered low :
    " This Fay is beauty's pride,
And such should grace the ardent glow
    Of elves that near me glide."

The Elf, in rapture, bent the knee
    Before the beauteous Fay :
But, turning from him haughtily,
    She cried : " Ye Powers ! obey

THE ELVES' GROTTO.

This magic pearl the Gnome King gave!
  His parting gift to me,
A talisman of might to save
  From foes of proud degree!"
She cast the jewel on the ground
  Before the royal throne,—
There came a mystic, hollow sound,
  That shook the lucent zone:
A chasm opened, and the pearl
  Was seized by wizard hand,
While lambent flames, in sparkling whirl,
  The precious treasure fanned!
Entranced, the jealous Fairy viewed
  The ruddy vapours' glow:
Then feared her sister's pride subdued,
  And tears commenced to flow.—
A voice resounded: "Fay, descend!
  Nor dread the fiery way;
The Elf King's power is at an end,
  Where Gnomes assert their sway!"

The Fay, in terror, viewed the flames,
   And, sorrowing, cried: "Alas!
I dare not, since the Gnome King claims
   My hand, his kingdom pass!"
Three times the voice responded: " Come!"
   And then the wizard hand
Swift vanished with the pearl:—though dumb
   With fright, the elfin band
Addressed the Monarch to prevent
   Such breach of ancient peace,
And warn these Powers of punishment,
   Unless such terrors cease !
The Elf King sat, revolving well
   The weird and hostile scene,
And watched the bride, whose fearful spell
   He heard with noble mien.
The Fay implored the King to yield,
   And cause these woes to end:
Her calling on the gnomes for shield
   Could not this prayer commend.

THE ELVES' GROTTO.

The Monarch bade his courtiers bring
   Fair censers, bright with gold;
And, bidding them sweet incense fling,
   His magic scrolls unrolled.
He then invoked the gnomes, by all
   Their ancient, plighted oath,
To keep their faith, nor rudely call
   For war to blight them both!
The elves resume the merry dance,
   While brilliant lights unfold
The cavern's fragile veils that glance
   From arches tipped with gold;
The glorious aisles in beauty glow,
   And rainbow colors rare
Array the glistening walls, that show
   A pearly lustre fair.—
The Fay, despairing, gazed on high,
   Then, floating to the dome,
Became a crystal butterfly,
   And found a radiant home!

The Elf despaired to break the charm,
  And prayed her love in vain :
While elves and fays, in mute alarm,
  Dissolved their mazy chain.
The Monarch charged the lover lorn
  To seek her isle, afar,
And bring her friends, with him to mourn
  This lost, effulgent star :
" Her sisters' prayers may soothe the Fay,
  Or thou must win renown,
And bring some talisman that may
  Subdue thy charmer's frown ! "

While yet they wondered at the scene,
  So weirdly new, and strange,
A murmur ran, the aisles between,
  Of some approaching change :
A champion, from the Gnome King's realm,
  Rode in on fiery steed ;

Before the throne he doffed his helm,
    And bade the King take heed:
"My master sends thee challenge true
    To meet him in the fight,
When thou thy cruel course shalt rue,
    And free this fairy bright!"
The King responded: "Tell the Gnome,
    I'll send a champion bold
To bravely seek him, o'er the foam,
    Before an hour is old."
The knightly messenger replied:
    "My master thee defies:
In rank with thee he ever vied:
    Thy throne shall be his prize!"
He cast his gauntlet on the ground,
    It gleamed with jewels rare:
The youthful Elf, with joyous bound,
    Swift floated through the air,
Then plucked the gauntlet up, with pride,
    And said: "My gracious King,

137

I fight the Gnome who thee defied,
    Whatever Fate may bring!"
The champion gnome, in high disdain,
    Replied: "My master proud
But challenges thy Monarch vain,
    And not the courtier crowd!"·
With that, his courser pawed the ground,
    The opening rocks received
The haughty gnome, while fire around
    Showed Earth's proud bosom heaved.

The Court drew near to bid the Elf
    His valor true display,
And bring the gnome a slave, himself,
    That should their King obey;
The Monarch said: "Thy trusty blade
    Must battle wage for me;
With armor true, the fays will aid
    Thy prowess, o'er the sea."

THE ELVES' GROTTO.

The Elf sped o'er the waves of light,
   And sought the coral isle
Where glow the vales supremely bright,
   That fairy griefs beguile.
"O loveliest Fay!" he dreaming said,
   As swiftly flew his car,
" Why hast thou from thy lover fled,
   That he should roam afar?
Unless I win thy precious love,
   And claim thee for my bride,
I 'll seek our crystal dome above,
   And perish by thy side:
A sparkling wonder shall enshrine
   This heart, that beats for thee ;
Entranced by thy fair charms divine,
   No waking morn I 'll see ;
But first I will the Gnome King meet,
   And soon avenge the slight
My Sovereign feels: the Gnome shall greet
   An earnest foe to-night!"

A troop of lovely fays received
 The valiant, elfin sprite.
And, while they for their sister grieved,
 Devised a plan of might:
They bade him seek her favorite grot.
 And bring a wondrous gem
The Fairy called "Forget-me-not."
 And swift the wavelets stem:
" The Gnome King guards the spot:" they cried.
 " And, fighting for thy King.
Thou wilt perhaps deserve thy bride:
 Then haste, with rapid wing!"
The Elf admired the brilliant plan,
 And blessed the fairies kind.
Then vowed, until that strife began.
 To wish no peace of mind:
They placed within his wondrous car
 A suit of armor gay,
And bade him wear it. when afar,
 To shield him in the fray.

140

THE ELVES' GROTTO.

The elfin lover hies through groves
    Of mango, palm and spice.
To seek the gem, and bravely roves
    Through glades, and fields of rice:
Strange goblins play, like starry gleams.
    Between the stately palms;
And weird enchantments throng his dreams,
    Till hope his spirit calms.
The moon is veiled like Eastern Queen:
    But 't is a glorious sight
To view the brilliants' dazzling sheen
    Across the breast of Night:
The Southern Cross flames on her brow,
    And planets shine as fair,
That glitter like twin diamonds, now,
    Upon her ebon hair.
The Elf invades the fairy dell.
    Though gnomes hurl javelin spines
From orange boughs, with wizard spell.
    To guard their gleaming mines:

The fire-flies speed on to light
　　The jungle's dreamy lane,
While peeping stars smile o'er his flight,
　　And bid him still his pain.
He hears the distant waterfalls
　　Leap down the mountain's side,
In playful song, that e'er recalls
　　His fair, enchanted bride :
Before him floats a vision sweet
　　On perfumed wings of air.
That seems his wandering course to greet,
　　And leads with warblings rare ;
Soft zephyrs fan his fevered brow,
　　And promise him their aid,
For deadly combat threatens, now,
　　Beyond the jungle's shade.
At length, within a wondrous vale
　　Where palms droop verdant plumes,
He sees the gleam of coat-of-mail
　　A grot's pale light illumes :

THE ELVES' GROTTO.

"The Gnome King still defends the place
   My love has left;" he thought,
"A sentry proud, who turns his face
   As though some foe he sought."
He bade his mystic car abide
   The issue of the fight;
And, leaping down, with youthful pride,
   Soon donned his armor bright:
The angel-fish had formed each scale
   Of purest azure hue;
The emerald trogon's plumes avail
   To deck his helmet true;
The bright macaw's gay. shining down
   Was plucked to weave his vest;
His visor gleaming rubies crown,
   Beneath his nodding crest:
A magic shield he bravely bore,
   And drew a diamond blade,
His Monarch's gift in days of yore,
   For rendering knightly aid.—

143

The Gnome King wooed the gentle Fay ;
   And, when she left her grot
To view the elves' wild revels gay,
   He sought the cherished spot ;
And loved to linger where she dwelt,
   To kiss the jewels bright
She gathered : while his heart would melt
   With lover-like delight.
Her favorite gem, she found beside
   A bubbling, silver well ;
But he had placed it there with pride,
   To grace her verdant dell ;
He guarded it with golden lance,
   And, when the Elf drew near,
Cast many a haughty, angry glance,
   And shook his glittering spear.—
The red flamingo gave its wing
   To form his scarlet dress ;
His shark-skin mail, of many a ring,
   Was forged by sorceress ;

144

THE ELVES' GROTTO.

The nautilus his helmet gave,
    'T was decked with heron's plume :
His shield of pearl, the briny wave
    Had taught him to assume. —
" Avaunt!" he shouted, "truant Elf,
    The Fay implores my aid :
Her sacred grot I guard, myself,
    Then quit this fairy glade ! "
The gallant Elf replied : " The gem
    I seek, to win her love,
Once graced thy royal diadem :
    But, in the stars above,
Where we may, all, our fates survey,
    I read a victor's crown :
And see I soon shall bear away
    The prize, despite thy frown !
I fight, a champion for my King,
    Whom thou hast so defied ;
While swift to combat bold I spring
    To win from thee my bride !

I here defy thee with this blade!"—
   'T was shaped by magic skill,
And powers of air its stroke obeyed
   To work the Gnome King ill!—
The foe was brave: he met the Elf
   In fatal contest now,
And, like a warrior, roused himself
   To fight, with threatening brow!
They fiercely wrestled, while the Gnome
   His utmost strength essayed:
He battled for the fairy's home:
   The Elf invoked her aid.
The gnomes desert their treasured gold
   To view the combat grim;
And aid full well their Monarch bold,
   Whose hopes are growing dim:
Enraged, to find the diamond blade
   Repel his mighty blows,
He shook his lance, and flames arrayed
   The point, while smoke arose!

THE ELVES' GROTTO.

The zephyrs blew the fire away,
  And quenched, with cooling dew,
The glowing spear, till wild dismay
  To fiercer battle drew :
He now threw fiery serpents round
  That fought the Elf with rage ;
But, with his magic blade, they found
  No power could engage :
For well he braved the wondrous lance,
  And, with the gleaming sweep
Of his weird sword's unerring glance,
  His foes at bay could keep :
He wounded them with many a blow :
  His sabre, flashing bright,
Could blind the Gnome, and proudly show
  Its lord the victor knight :
At length his rival flies afar !
  And now the joyous sprite
Has won the prize, and turns his car
  With airy, rapid flight.—

Soft beamed the moon across the main,
  With brilliant path of light:
And flying-fish, in glimmering chain,
  Leaped high, with hasty fright,
As swept the gleaming car along
  The trembling, silver sea;
While water-nymphs, in choral song,
  Breathed tender melody.—
But, swift as glides the magic car,
  The Elf, whose hopes seem bright,
Would fain outstrip the shooting-star,
  That mocks him through the night:
"Ye glorious lights of Heaven!" he cried,
  "That cheered me in my pain,
Oh, bring me to my loved one's side,
  Nor let my toils be vain!"—
The kindly fays had sought the grot
  To win their sister's heart,
And bid her yield, and trouble not
  Their love by subtle art;

But vain their prayers and anxious words,
   The crystal dome retained
The timid Fay, till, swift as birds,
   The grot her lover gained.
Before his Monarch's throne, he rears
   The beauteous gem on high
To bid the Fairy cease her fears,
   Nor from his pleadings fly:
"My liege!" he said, "we bravely fought;
   The Gnome King battled well;
He lost the victory he sought;
   Thy sword dissolved his spell!"—
He gazed upon the sparkling height,
   Where, 'mid fantastic forms,
The butterfly, his dreams' delight,
   Escaped from troublous storms:
"My love, my own, return to me!"
   He cried in pleading tones,
"Thy cherished gem I bring to thee,
   Then hear thy lover's moans!

Across the tropic sea I fled
　To seek thy early home;
Thy sisters' hearts in pity bled,
　They sought thee o'er the foam.
For thee I braved a gallant foe
　Who well deserved the fight;
But thy fair image nerved each blow,
　And soon he took to flight.
Then come, my life, my own!" he cried;
　"The Gnome King sighs in vain;
Return to me, my charming bride,
　And wear love's gentle chain!"—

The crystal phantom slowly fades,
　Till, from the dazzling height,
The Fairy floats, for love soon aids
　Her faithful pleader's might.
Her lovely face all blushing glowed,
　And eyes of heavenly blue

150

THE ELVES' GROTTO.

Looked down with softened light, that showed
    She prized his valor true.
The moonbeams spun her veil, 't was thrown
    Around an angel form ;
Her azure wings, more lustrous grown,
    And gentle glance, inform
Her raptured lover, that a knight
    Of such courageous mien
Is worthy of her beauty bright :
    She seems a radiant queen !

The Elfin Monarch, smiling, blessed
    The fairy lovers' tie ;
And, bending low, they each confessed
    His potent sovereignty.
A burst of weirdest music rolled
    Along the brilliant aisles,
Where elves poured tinkling showers of gold,
    That rose in gorgeous piles.

In gay procession round the throne,
　　The tricksy phantoms hied,
While flowers were bound, in perfumed zone,
　　Around the fairy bride:
"O conqueror of the mighty Gnome!"
　　The fairies sang with joy,
"Thy love no more will bid thee roam,
　　Nor should new strife employ
Thy steadfast courage: peace be thine,
　　And happiness untold:
Enjoy the hours that gaily twine
　　Their wreaths for heroes bold!"
The chariot wafts the lovers twain,
　　In dreams of joyous love,
To seek a grot beside the main,
　　The laughing waves above:
They dwell within that cavern fair,
　　Remote from mortal view,
Or sport, on wings of tropic air,
　　Across the waters blue.

THE GNOME KING'S WEDDING.

———

The Gnome King's palace gleams with gold,
  And jewels sparkling bright,
Where ruby columns, rare, uphold
  A dome of radiant light:
The topaz and the amethyst
  Are strewed to deck the floor:
While diamond arches, like a mist
  Of morn, superbly soar
In dreamy vistas, splendid aisles,
  All vaulted o'er with pearl,
Where sapphires glow like azure isles,
  And rainbow colors whirl!

When, flying from the victor Elf,
　　The Gnome King sought his throne,
Winged courtiers, wondering like himself,
　　With many a pitying moan,
Consoled their haughty, vanquished King,
　　And cursed the magic blade,
That could such wild disaster bring,
　　Despite their proffered aid.
His Champion grieved, that he had not
　　Waylaid the fatal sword,
Or seized it ere he left the grot,
　　And thus have saved his lord:
He knelt before the dazzling throne,
　　And made obeisance low,
Until his Sovereign's features shone,
　　As wonder banished woe!
"My gracious Master!" soft he said,
　　"But deign thy slave a word:
That blade hath well the Elf King sped,
　　Yet, should my prayer be heard,

THE GNOME KING'S WEDDING.

I soon will rend it from his knight,
    Who, rapt in bridal joys,
May soon forget its wizard might,
    While gnomes deserve such toys!
I will transform my warrior face,
    And, like a merry sprite,
Will seek the prize, with stealthy pace:
    The brand shall crown my flight!"
He looked around to see if all
    Approved his crafty speech:
The valiant gnomes now thronged the hall,
    And he inspired each:
The Court applauded, till the dome
    Resounded with their mirth.
The Monarch bade the faithful Gnome
    Now prove his noble worth:
" Return," he cried, " with that weird blade,
    And claim a kingly gift!
For he that grants me such an aid
    His shield may proudly lift!"

The Champion Gnome, with cunning art,
    Disguised his features bold:
And, playing his nefarious part,
    Soon left the realms of gold.
He sped across the azure sea,
    And sought the fairy grot,
Revolving, with a wily glee,
    How best to reach the spot.
But, as he passed a lovely isle,
    He saw the lovers twain,
Where forests spread for many a mile,
    Swift winging from the main:
In bridal happiness, the pair,
    He sought to injure now,
Soft floated through the balmy air:
    Then, with unruffled brow,
The Elf resigned his magic blade
    To please the charming bride,
And placed it 'neath a palm-tree's shade,
    His fairy love beside.

THE GNOME KING'S WEDDING.

The caitiff Gnome drew near to seize
   The precious, wizard gem:
And, like a snake between the trees,
   Crept round each tapering stem,
Till, when he deemed the treasure won,
   The noble Elf espied
The stranger's mien: and, like the sun
   That strikes the gleaming tide,
Smote down the baffled Gnome, and then
   Compelled his tardy flight,
Until, within a darksome den
   That never knew the light.
He chained him, near his Monarch's grot:
   And sped to warn the King,
That some mysterious counter-plot
   Had made this gnome take wing. —
His fairy bride soon floated o'er
   The golden, rolling tide,
And left her shell beside the shore,
   To reach her lover's side.

Her sister, who was full of hope
   To win the Gnome King's hand,
Still lingered,—as a further scope
   Her plans might yet demand,—
Beside the grotto's crystal arch:
   And, when she heard the Gnome
Bewail his fate's relentless march,
   Half sighed to think of home:
Then longed to break the charm that bound
   The mournful, captive sprite:
Till soon an entrance way she found,
   To reach the realm of Night.
Where, bound with fairy chains, she saw
   The haughty Gnome; and knew
It was the Champion, whom, with awe,
   She heard give challenge true.
"Art thou the hero knight," she said,
   "That late, on wondrous steed,
Defied the Elf King's power?   He fled
   The dangerous fight, indeed!

158

But his proud champion brings thee here
   In fetters harsh, to-day:
How nobly thou thy King wouldst cheer,
   And bear that brand away!"
The Gnome replied: " Most lovely fay!
   Hadst thou been called to reign,
These woes could not have found their way
   To dim thy jewelled train;
But learn the spell that binds my form,
   And set thy pleader free;
Then I will strive, through peace and storm,
   To deck a throne for thee!"

The jealous fay flew near the bride,
   To learn the magic charm,
By listening, when the Elf replied
   To questions of alarm,
How he could bind the Gnome so well:
   The laughing Elf declared.

No power on earth could break the spell.
   Till he its secret shared.
The Fay then sadly asked him, why
   He loved her charms no more :
She well deserved a kind reply,
   Who left her distant shore.
The Elf soft murmured : "Touch his wings,
   And breathe our Monarch's name :
Wouldst free him, say, 'The grace of kings!'
   Wouldst bind him, 'Rest in flame!'"
Enraptured, now, to hear the charm,
   The jealous sister left
The happy pair, who dreamed no harm,
   Of all their bliss bereft !
With hasty pace, she joyful sought
   The Gnome's enchanted cell,
And, with the sorcery thus taught,
   Dissolved the mighty spell !
The Gnome, on bended knee, replied,
   And vowed allegiance true :

THE GNOME KING'S WEDDING.

Then sought the magic prize: and hied
 Along the ocean blue,
Until he saw the bride display
 The brand's wild, flashing light,
And watch the Elf, as prone he lay
 In airy slumbers bright.
The Gnome appeared a gentle sprite,
 And almost feared the blade,
Until the bride, with fond delight,
 Seemed dreaming in the shade;
Approaching, with the faintest stir,
 He seized the brand, and sped
Through fiery ways: ambition's spur
 With visions charmed his head!

The jewelled halls are bright, to-day,
 With happiness untold;
The Gnome King wields a friendly sway
 Amid the aisles of gold:

And wingèd thousands throng around
  The sapphire throne of blue,
To swell the pæan's joyful sound,
  And hail the Champion true.
He bore the magic sword with pride,
  And strode the aisles along,
Where surged an all tumultuous tide
  Of fairy shout and song:
On bended knee he placed the blade
  Before the gorgeous throne;
The Monarch joyfully surveyed
  Its lustrous, emerald zone:
Then raised the wondrous brand on high,
  And, waving it around,
Said: "Elfin Powers, I ye defy!
  Your talisman is found!
Full well I know the mystic power
  The Elf King long has claimed,
But this good sword can ruin shower:
  My prowess it has shamed!

THE GNOME KING'S WEDDING.

And who can e'er resist our might,
  When, with our arms of flame,
This dreaded blade shall put to flight
  The foes of our proud name!
Assemble all our troops," he cried,
  " For sudden war, to-day !
Let broidered tents, in martial pride,
  Be pitched without delay ! "
With clashing shield and gleaming spear,
  The Gnomes replied : " Lead on ! "
But now his wizard might made clear
  A grievous woe, anon.
" The Elf King's magic scrolls forbid
  Our use of fire below."
He said, " or else our flames had hid
  His grot in fiery glow !
The sea, alone, is ours as well.
  And we must storm his fleet,
With all the means that rage can swell.
  To pledge his sure defeat ! "

The Champion Gnome, as Admiral,
   Was named to lead the fray,
While all held warlike carnival,
   And dared the realms of day.
With gilded mail, of every hue,
   The courtiers then arrayed
Their glistening forms, and grand review
   Of all their arms was made.
The Gnome King ordered slaves to seek
   The deep abyss below,
And bid the flames their worst to wreak,
   To whelm the elves with woe,
By rising 'neath the mighty deep,
   With fierce, volcanic power,
Where'er the foemen's fleet might sweep,
   Before the battle's hour.
"Our vessels quickly must be framed,"
   He said, " of shining pearl,
With golden masts, and war proclaimed,
   That we may bravely hurl

THE GNOME KING'S WEDDING.

Our navy, with resistless might,
   Upon the Elfin fleet:
Before the twilight ushers night,
   Their King shall own defeat!
Our Champion shall defy the churl,
   As late he did so well:
Then haste, our banners' sheen unfurl:
   Let trumpets loudly swell!"
A phalanx proud, of warriors bold,
   Obeyed the martial call,
And helmets waved their crests of gold
   Along the jewelled hall:
The Gnome King led his army bright
   From out the realms of ore,
And soon encamped them, for the fight,
   Around a coral shore.
By mystic art, the fleet soon rose
   Beside the tranquil sea,
And, ere the early morning's close,
   Was manned, by proud decree!

The bridegroom Elf awoke from dreams
    Of happiness, to find,
That, while he quaffed Hope's golden streams,
    His fate had proved unkind.
The fairy bride lamented o'er
    A loss supremely great:
But what disturbed her lover more,
    And made him meditate,
Was, who had stolen the precious blade:
    He sought the darksome cell,
And found no prisoner in its shade:
    The Gnome had prospered well!—
The Elf King quickly learned the tale;
    But, by his magic art,
Could all the mystery unveil
    And sage advice impart:
"The Gnome has borne the trusty blade
    To his great Sovereign's realm;
Who now, I see, will soon invade
    Our coasts: lest they o'erwhelm

166

THE GNOME KING'S WEDDING.

Our prowess, swift, the fleet prepare !
   I name thee to command :
My art shall save us from despair :
   The talismanic brand,
Their prize, will not obey the Gnome
   When wielded in the fray ;
And we shall drive their navy home
   In terrible dismay ! "

The Elf assumed command with speed,
   And soon arrayed the fleet :
The Eltin host was vast, indeed,
   And never knew defeat :
But all bethought them of the blade,
   The Gnome King proudly bore :
Yet trusted in their Sovereign's aid,
   And boldly left the shore.
The shining wavelets danced around
   The silvery sails and oars ;

While trumpets blew, with joyful sound,
  The pennons waved in scores!
But first, the King adjured the deep:
  For strange, volcanic might
Began, beneath the waves, to creep,
  And threatened instant flight!
The waters boiled, and flames arose:
  Till, with enchantment's power,
The Monarch wrought a wondrous close
  To storms that seemed to lower:
Upon a gilded deck he sat.
  And charmed the waves, below,
With such a potent magic, that
  They quenched their fiery flow!
The sea grew calm, the sails were spread:
  And soon the Gnome King's bark
Appeared— a mighty squadron's head—
  With purple sails, to mark
Where'er their leader should engage
  The hated Elfin ships:

168

For, filled with an imperial rage,
　That Monarch pressed his lips,
To see the hostile fleet evade
　The terrors he prepared,
And ready now to dare the blade
　Whose might he had declared.
He turned to greet the Champion Gnome,
　And said : " Our foes make light
Of Powers that should have turned the foam
　To fiery surges bright :
Engage with their weird Monarch's ship :
　His pennon's haughty gleam
Shall soon, dishonored, lowly dip,
　While mine shall proudly stream!"
The faithful Gnome replied : "Great King!
　Thy arms shall conquest win :
But, ere to battle's proof we wing,
　Bethink thee how within
The Elf King's power that brand had stayed,
　Had not the dark-eyed Fay,

With mystic arts, for thee betrayed
    The secret of their sway:
Oh, could I see her reign with thee:
    That radiant hall of ours
Should hail the Queen that set me free,
    And strew her throne with flowers!"

The Monarch praised the kindly Gnome;
    For, since the Elf had wed
The lovely sister, his fair dome
    Should greet this Fay, instead.
"A truce to talk of bridal joys;"
    He cried, "and swift press on;
The Elf King's might all peace destroys;
    When victory comes, anon,
We will relate those charms divine;
    But honor beeks away:
A victor's crown shall soon be mine;
    Then brave that proud array!"

THE GNOME KING'S WEDDING.

The Champion Gnome, as admiral,
   Gave orders for the fight;
It seemed a brilliant festival:
   For every ship was dight
With fairy colors, gold and gems;
   But, when the trumpet blew,
The monarchs doffed their diadems
   For helmets, proved and true:
While every elf and gnome prepared
   To wield the fearful powers
They could command, and bravely shared
   The dangers of those hours.
With grappling hooks, the vessels paired
   For deadly combat now:
Winged heroes strode the decks, that dared
   The leap, as, prow to prow,
The ships with warlike onset shook;
   And knights to battle flew,
With glittering lance and shield, to brook
   The worst the foe could do.

The Gnome King's ship, with purple sail,
    Soon reached its rival bark :
Like birds that fly before the gale,
    They swept to conflict dark :
With jacinth blades, the gnomes and elves
    Soon battled for the prize ;
The gnomes, from charms to free themselves :
    The elves to signalize
Their valor, and repel the foe
    That marred their ancient peace.
The Gnome King viewed the combat's glow,
    And saw the strife increase :
Then drew the mighty brand, and cleft
    The sunny air with pride,
To dare the Elf King, as bereft
    Of all his power beside.
The gallant Elf desired to meet
    The Royal Gnome once more,
And triumph, if he could defeat
    That rival as before :

172

THE GNOME KING'S WEDDING.

His King replied: "The talisman
 Will own its lord in me;'
Then I will lead, in danger's van:
 But, when I once can free
Thy valor from its dangerous might.
 Advance, and win the day:
Thou art the hero of the fight.
 And all shall thee obey!"

The King moved on to meet the Gnome,
 Who boldly raised the sword:
It flashed across the glistening foam,
 Then drooped before its lord:
Enraged, the Gnome King bravely sought
 To raise it for the fray,
But, leaping with the speed of thought,
 It weirdly sped away,
And sought the Elf King's gracious side:
 He kissed the blade with joy.

173

Then gave it to his champion tried,
　　Who well could it employ.
The gnomes, in terror, thronged around,
　　And newly armed their King;
Till he, for courage long renowned,
　　Defiance bold could fling.

The Elf advanced with deadly stroke,
　　And cleft a gleaming way,
Where, wrapped in flames and cloud of smoke,
　　The Gnome King sought to sway
The terrors of the fight; but soon,—
　　Though fierce the flames he blew,—
The Elf, beneath the blazing noon,
　　Well proved his valor true;
The talisman, in wondrous sweep,
　　Surpassed the utmost power
The Gnome could bring by witchcraft deep;
　　And conquest crowned the hour!

174

THE GNOME KING'S WEDDING.

The Elf King sounded trumpets now,
    For parley with the Gnome;
And soon they met upon the prow,
    Above the sparkling foam:
The warriors then for peace agreed.
    And signals were displayed:
A stately marriage was decreed:
    The brilliant, dark-eyed maid,
Who loved the Gnome, should wedded be,
    When all the Powers would meet
For joyous, bridal revelry,
    And soon forget defeat.
· The Gnome King owned love's gentle power,
    And praised his victor's sway;
While many a knight beguiled the hour
    With honors of the fray.
The conquering elves sailed home, to seek
    Their brightest, festal gear:
The gnomes withdrew, although with pique.
    And sought their richest cheer.

The palace beams with fairy lights!
  Beside the Monarch's throne,
Another orb of gems invites
  A Queen to claim her own.
The fairy sisters cross the sea,
  In pleasure barks of pearl,
While all the elves, in joyous glee,
  Their silken sails unfurl;
The argosy sweeps o'er the main
  To reach a verdant shore;
There valiant knights, in gallant train,
  Receive the fays once more.
A bridal pageant soon is formed,
  To seek the palace, where
A mystic rite will be performed,
  That all the gnomes can share:
A pontiff of the sacred fire
  Awaits their gallant King,
While warble soft the glorious choir,
  That heavenly music sing.

176

THE GNOME KING'S WEDDING.

The Gnome King soared to greet the fays:
    And soon the blushing bride
Acknowledged how she loved to praise
    His valor, that defied
Such mighty magic in the fray:
    He kissed her glowing cheek,
And vowed that ever, from that day,
    He would devoutly seek
Her happiness above his own!
    The lovely sister Fay
Smiled tenderly, and brightly shone
    In bridal samite gay.

The Elf and Gnome were reconciled;
    And all moved proudly on
To where the choristers beguiled
    Their princely march: anon,
Adorned with robes of awful state,
    The Pontiff met the pair,

177

FAIRY TALES OF THE TROPICS.

Before the radiant palace-gate,
  And blessed the perfumed air.
While clouds of incense rise on high,
  They seek an altar fair,
Where flames the fire to sanctify
  The vows they fondly share :
Along the diamond aisles they move :
  And now the sacred flames
The Pontiff's noble prayer approve,
  And bless the royal names.

With grand array, the Elf King came
  To view the pageant gay :
His wingèd warriors could claim
  The glory of the day :
But all declared, this gladsome feast
  Surpassed their wildest dream,
And praised the stately, ancient priest,
  Whose blessing seemed supreme.

THE GNOME KING'S WEDDING.

The talisman, that won the fight,
　　Was borne before the King,
And viewed by many a hardy knight,
　　That feared its deadly swing.
Beside the Gnome King's throne was reared
　　His rival's dazzling seat:
Where soon that kindly Monarch cheered
　　The gnomes with praises meet.
The bridal pair were then enthroned;
　　And now the Pontiff placed
The crown, her sister had disowned,
　　Upon the brow it graced.
In joyful concord, gnomes and fays
　　Did homage to the Queen:
And festivals, for many days,
　　Were held with joy serene:
On rainbow wings the hours flew by,
　　While through the realms of gold
The fairies roamed, to beautify
　　A wealth of gems untold:

179

The palace rang with joyous mirth,
    And, near the sapphire throne,
Where blazing brilliants bound its girth,
    The brides in splendor shone :
The royal Gnome each wish divined,
    And, with his gracious Queen,
Enhanced the wonders he combined
    In aisles of jewelled sheen.
The sisters cherished harmony;
    While gnomes and elves became
The truest allies : jubilee
    Was held in domes of flame.
The elves returned to deck their grot :
    But oft, at sunset hour,
They seek a well-remembered spot,—
    Secure in magic power, —
And hail the gnomes as brother sprites :
    The fleets unite in glee,
And heroes chant immortal fights,
    Around the gleaming sea !

THE QUEEN OF THE FAIRIES.

———

A land of mountains, rising high
  In glorious, sylvan pride,
Where palms and orange-blossoms vie
  With fountains sparkling wide:
There, rivers leap, with silvery glance,
  Adown the cliffs sublime,
While Phœbus hurls his brightest lance
  To stay the flight of Time :
A fairy city gilds the air,
  Beside the rippling sea,
In glowing beauty, weird and rare,
  From every trouble free !

181

The Fairy Queen, that ruled alone
   This Paradise of light,
Through all the tropic isles was known,
   And every elfin knight
Desired to win her favour: yet
   In vain they nobly strove:
The Queen could not her rank forget,
   Howe'er their plans they wove:
In flower of early, blooming grace,
   Sweet love was all unknown:
And, when they praised her beaming face,
   She bade them leave her throne.
The Elf King, only, seemed to please:
   But he, engrossed in thought,
Scarce visited these distant seas,
   While proudest deeds he wrought:
His fame through fairy land was known,
   And, from each dreamy shore,
Kings visited Earth's palmy zone
   To hear his wondrous lore.

THE QUEEN OF THE FAIRIES.

Full joyfully the years rolled on
    Amid the coral isles:
Where elves and gnomes had warred, anon
    Blithe Hope's enchanting smiles
Adorned each day with promised bliss:
    Till checked by rumored tales,
That wizard guards had been remiss
    While swept the Eastern gales.
The Fairy Queen's fair, distant land,
    Where she in beauty reigned
Along the mighty ocean's strand,
    Had strangely been profaned:
The winds had borne a daring race
    Of Genii o'er the sea:
From Afric shores they came apace,
    To rule those islands free;
Their legions swept the trembling air,
    That flamed before their course,
While fairy nations, in despair,
    Bemoaned their tyrant force!

Although the Queen had rarely seen
    The Elf King's noble air,
She ever praised a knightly mien
    That seemed new foes to dare ;
And strange disaster threatened now.
    Since evil spirits came
On wings of cloud, with wicked vow,
    To wrap the isles in flame.
Her loving fairies thronged around
    The pearly palace-gate
To pray the Queen, for wit renowned,
    To save them from a fate
Appalling e'en to sprites, or send
    The King an embassy,
That should their direful state commend
    And urge a piteous plea.
The brilliant Fairy Queen replied :
    " Since peril threatens now,
Embassadors shall cross the tide,
    And all our cause avow ;

For every Island Power must rise
   To check the dreadful foe
That, sweeping from the Eastern skies,
   Has filled our land with woe.
The great Enchanter, that resides
   Within our happy realm,
Shall bring the Elf King: who divides
   With him the power to whelm
Our foes in raging seas of fire :
   But our Magician great
Must first arrest our foemen's ire,
   That would o'erwhelm our State."
She bade her courtiers seek the cave
   Where dwelt the Seer old,
Beside the glowing, Southern wave,
   And all her plan unfold :
The Queen revered the wisdom deep
   For which he well was famed :
His magic charmed the surges' sweep,
   And oft the lightnings tamed.

The fairies sought the dreamy vale
    Enchanted by his spell ;
Though loth to greet the vernal gale,
    He left his ancient cell.—
Before the Queen he bowed the knee,
    And prayed her kindle fires
Along the hills that touched the sea.
    Then watch the flaming pyres :
Until the Genii should perceive
    The light, and dream brave arms
Were ready foemen to receive.
    And cease their loud alarms.
The flames leaped up along the shore,
    As though in proud disdain :
And soon a car of dragons bore
    Their master o'er the main.
The Wizard sought the Elfin grot,
    Where council grave was held :
They called the Gnome King to the spot,
    Who oft in war excelled.

The noble allies then agreed
  To lead their armies brave,
And follow, with all knightly speed.
  Across the gleaming wave.
The great Enchanter shook his locks,
  Which thought had touched with white,
And said: "I guard our island rocks.
  Through vigils of the night,
With fires to mock the Genii's arms,
  As though a mighty force
Were marshalled, by our potent charms.
  Where trumpets mutter hoarse:
But soon their spies may learn the truth.
  And then our mountains fair
No more will guard eternal youth.
  When fays new chains will wear:
Thy troops should cross the wave with me,
  Or else, most mighty King.
My car shall bear thee o'er the sea
  With swiftest dragon's wing;

Then, by thy art, we may contrive
    To stem this torrent's might,
And, when thy armies vast arrive,
    Shall put the foe to flight!"
The Monarch deemed this judgment good,
    And bade his favorite Elf,
Who war's array well understood,
    To lead the hosts, himself;
But when the gnomes for battle came,
    Their Chieftain would command,
Until the Elf King should proclaim
    The hour for conflict grand.
The Elfin knights assembled round,
    When swelled the trumpet's call,
And hailed the stirring, martial sound,
    That sent a thrill through all:
The Gnome King hastened to prepare
    His fleet, and warriors brave:
While every hero longed to share
    These perils o'er the wave.

THE QUEEN OF THE FAIRIES.

The dragons swiftly bore the King,
  And their Enchanter old,
Upon the balmy gales of Spring,
  To where they might behold
The Genii gathered for the fray,
  Along an endless plain,
In frowning ranks, with proud display,
  Beside the silvery main.
They towered, as to reach the skies,
  A gloomy phalanx bold,
And seemed all rivals to despise,
  In numbers vainly told.
Their Sultan's tent was formed of clouds,
  Of gorgeous rainbow dyes;
His satraps brave, in brilliant crowds,
  Were Afrites, tried and wise;
They left their native shore to seek
  New haunts across the sea,
And brought an army fierce, to wreak
  Their vengeance on the free.

The Elf King and Enchanter rode
  Along the mountain heights,
And viewed the fires that brightly glowed;
  Then, with mysterious lights,
Deceived the Genii, till they deemed
  The mountains filled with foes,
And closer drew their lines, and seemed
  To dare them to disclose
Their warlock garrison; but now,
  While trumpets answering blew,
The King, upon the mountain's brow,
  Displayed enchantments new:
Strange phantoms seemed to pace the heights,
  In forms of giant size,
And armed as though colossal knights,
  That guarded some fair prize.
The Genii gathered round their King,
  And marvelled at the scene;
For dragons came, on fiery wing,
  And dashed their ranks between:

190

That Monarch sent a herald bold
  To summon down the foe,
Where stretched the plain for miles untold,
  To render blow for blow.
The Afrite, who advanced with pride,
  Was clad in tiger skin,
A golden trumpet by his side,
  That parley might begin :
He sounded thrice, and silence fell
  Along the hills and vales ;
Then shouted to a sentinel
  Across the quiet dales.
The old Enchanter rose to meet
  The sound of martial tread,
And, with his dragons, swept to greet
  The Afrite's pinions red.
The herald's wings, of sanguine hue,
  Were folded by his side,
While boldly now his trump he blew,
  And thus the King defied :

" From Afric shores we come," he said.
　" To dwell within this isle,
All foes before our march have fled,
　As ye shall soon, awhile:
Submit to our imperial yoke,
　And ye will wrath dispel:
But they new terrors will invoke
　Whoever dare rebel!"
He gazed in scorn upon the foe,
　Expecting all would fly,
And thus prevent an idle blow,
　When might like his drew nigh.
The grave Enchanter answered well:
　" I bear thy terms severe
To our fair Sovereign's citadel,
　Who graciously will hear
Whate'er is righteous; but, until
　I come with her reply.
Let royal truce thy words fulfil,
　Or we your arms defy!"

The Afrite viewed the phantoms stride
　　Along the frowning heights,
Where wizard armies seemed to glide
　　As flames illumed their rites.
He said : "Our mighty master will
　　Allow thy humble prayers :
But let thy words new fears instil--
　　No foes escape our snares."
The great Enchanter wished for time
　　To bring the elves and gnomes,
In numbers vast, from every clime,
　　To guard these fairy homes.
He said : "Withdraw your army grand,
　　While I will seek the Queen:"
Then gave his dragons proud command,
　　And sought the sky serene.
Full well he knew that none would yield;
　　And urged his wondrous car,
To warn the Monarch who could wield
　　Brave legions from afar.

He soon rejoined the Elfin King:
　　Then, borne on wings of flame,
They reached the palace gate, to bring
　　Their scheme and truce proclaim.

A sound of fairy music swelled
　　Across the moonlit sea,
Where sailed the fleets, their charms compelled,
　　Beside the King's decree:
With panoply of war there came
　　The Gnome King's ship of pearl;
His standard was a golden flame,
　　That streamed in mystic whirl.
The fleet soon anchored off the port,
　　Beside the silver stairs,
Where gathered all the splendid court,
　　Relieved from anxious cares.
The Fairy Queen came down to greet
　　Her brave defenders well,

THE QUEEN OF THE FAIRIES.

.Rejoiced the Elfin King to meet.
   Who could their fate foretell.
She sat upon a ruby throne.
   Beside the waters blue.
While warriors, in a shining zone,
   Avowed their fealty true.
The old Enchanter knelt before
   The lovely Fairy's feet.
And said: " My Sovereign, we adore
   Thy goodness, and entreat
A kind attention to the plan
   The Elf King will unfold:
No wiser Monarch e'er began
   A war with outlaws bold."

All hailed the hero of the scene,
   And longed to hear his voice.
As, clad in mail of dazzling sheen.
   His smile made all rejoice.

The Elf King viewed the Fairy Queen,
  Whose beauty charmed his heart,
And, with a gallant, courteous mien,
  Began: "I will impart
To thee, crowned sister, how this strife
  Should best conducted be;
For well I trust, while we have life,
  No foe to liberty
Within our ranks will dare arise
  To court these Genii fierce,
Whose mocking words we may despise,
  Until their ranks we pierce.
Our best enchantments are required
  To meet their onset wild;
But mystic arts I have acquired
  That foes have oft beguiled;
The noble Gnome will bid the flames
  Arise beneath their tread,
While I defeat their lofty aims
  Where mountains rise o'erhead;

THE QUEEN OF THE FAIRIES.

My elves shall aid me guard the heights,
  The fleet will watch the sea,
While dragons soar, with daring flights,
  To keep the heavens free."
The Queen responded: "Mighty King,
  Thy prowess well is known,
And terror wide thy arms will bring
  To guard my peaceful throne:
But I must tremble for thee still,
  For such all-dangerous foes
Were never known, and all thy skill
  Will scarcely ward their blows:
And thou, most gallant Gnome, beware!
  Thy flames must breathe surprise:
For Eblis sends these shapes of air
  That seek our happy skies."
She looked, with an approving smile,
  Where, decked in armor bright
Of scarlet hue, he leaned the while
  Upon a sword of might.

The Gnome King answered: "Gracious Queen!
  The flames obey me well;
But I must haste, these rocks between,
  And seek a fiery cell,
Where I will all my power assert,
  Whene'er the signal-call
Shall bid my slaves their might exert
  Within Earth's flaming hall:
My Champion will the force divide,
  And guard our flanks by sea,
While I repair, the fire to guide,
  Where none may follow me."
He struck the ground, and vanished soon; —
  And now the Elfin King
Declared the truce must end by noon:
  Then bade his army bring
Their gallant force to guard the mount
  Where phantom sentries moved:
The Champion Gnome would there recount
  His plans, while he approved.

They seek the mount, and soon combine
  The manner of the fight:
The fleet should sweep, in glittering line,
  To watch the Genii's flight:
If they audaciously should strive
  To gain the palace fair,
Cloud signals would the war revive
  And bid the elves beware.
The Monarch bade the sprites prepare
  The mountains for the fray,
By piling trees, in high mid-air,
  In terrible array.
By potent spells, their powers availed
  To guard the summits well:
That, wheresoe'er the Genii scaled,
  With shout, and purpose fell,
The Elfin cohorts should roll down
  Their avalanches vast
From off the rocky summits' crown,
  Like rushing of the blast.

Day dawned while yet they bravely toiled :
   And now the Genii's camp
Resounded, as the Afrites spoiled
   The plain, where vapours damp
Arose to veil their ardor fierce,
   And rent the trees with scorn,
To wield the forests that should pierce
   Their way that sullen morn.

The peace was o'er, and now the foe,
   In shining columns dense,
Advanced, as when the deserts glow
   With moving shafts immense :
Their ranks extended o'er the plain
   In masses, vast and grim,
With flashing wings, while fierce disdain
   Could not such grandeur dim,
A giant host the forests bore,
   And up the rocky steep

THE QUEEN OF THE FAIRIES.

They proudly rose, their King before,
    Beside a river's leap
That swept the heights with rush and roar:
    Then halted to prepare
A dreadful onset; and, with more
    Than courage, rent the air
With demon shouts to awe the foe:
    While their majestic King
Arrayed them for a deadly blow,
    And furled each scarlet wing;
His eyes were lightnings, and his voice
    In thunder seemed to roll,
As now he bade his slaves rejoice,
    And storm their mountain-goal!

The mighty Genii grandly braved
    The dark and rugged way:
The Elf King then his sceptre waved,
    To daunt the vast array:—

With crash and din, came rolling down
   The avalanches dread,
And, heeding not the Genii's frown,
   Swept through their legions' head.
They halted, then pressed on amain,
   And hurled the woods on high,
As though, with impious courage vain,
   To reach the vaulted sky;
But, undismayed by crash of trees,
   With hurtling bough and limb,
The Elf King bade his ally seize
   The power decreed to him :—
And burning streams of lava red
   Poured down the heights sublime :
The fiery rivers grandly sped :
   'T was their appointed time!
The Afrites cleft the flaming way :
   But mystic Geysers rose,
And whelmed their ranks, till new dismay
   Dispirited their blows :

THE QUEEN OF THE FAIRIES.

They then retreated to the plain,
   Where counsel, weird and grave,
Was held till eve: for all in vain
   Appeared their onset brave.

The Elf King saw their plan, and called
   The Wizard, old and wise,
With his great ally, and forestalled
   The foe's wild enterprise:
" The Genii threaten dangers new: "
   He said, " to-morrow's sun
Will see them cloud the welkin blue,
   But not our arms to shun.
They come as powers of the air:
   And thou, Magician true,
Must bring a host of dragons there
   That shall the fight renew:
Our warriors will these coursers ride,
   And, with their wings of fire,

Our arms shall crush the Genii's pride,
    Howe'er they may aspire."

Within the fairy palace, joy
    Was blent that eve with fear;
The beauteous Queen could not employ
    Her thoughts within the sphere
She graced, and said: "My noble friends
    Have warred this day to save
My kingdom; and, since Night descends
    Across the moonlit wave,
My crescent car, in beamy guise,
    Shall bear me to the camp,
To see the host of elves arise
    From mountain mosses damp."
She bade her chosen fairies ride
    Winged coursers in her train,
While all the court, with joyous pride,
    Flew near her glowing rein.—

THE QUEEN OF THE FAIRIES.

The dreamy pageant rose on high,
   And sought the mountains fair,
To greet the army of the sky,
   And grateful bliss to share.
The Elfin myriads rose to meet
   The gracious Fairy Queen:
And heroes knelt before her feet,
   While she, in starry sheen,
Declared them knights, and praised their deeds:
   She prayed the King receive
Her thanks, and urge his dragon steeds,
   Lest foemen should retrieve
Their loss when morning shed its light:
   Then turned her magic car,
And left the warriors in delight,
   To seek her throne afar.
The gallant elves prepared to meet
   The Afrites' pinions wide,
And dragons crouched before their feet
   To soar with heroes tried.

205

The morning dawned, and o'er the plain
   Appeared a wondrous sight :
The Genii rose in cloudy train,
   Whose wings threw shades of night :
Their King was crowned with rays of light,
   And hurled the lightnings dread,
While thunders rolled around his flight,
   And flame glowed 'neath his tread :
His wings were vast, and drove the wind,
   That rushed in gales away ;
His serpent locks shot fire behind,
   His glance defied the day :
He led his legions through the air
   To take the frowning heights :—
A dauntless host soon brought despair,
   They soared in awful flights.
The Elf King rode a dragon bold,
   Whose wings eclipsed the sun,
While fiery waves around it rolled,
   And clouds of vapours dun :

THE QUEEN OF THE FAIRIES.

That Monarch bore a lance of flame,
    And, with his armies brave,
Assailed the Genii as they came
    His country to enslave:
The dragon's scales resisted all
    The lightning's angry power,
His burning breath could well appal
    These demons of the hour:
The Elf King boldly met the foe,
    And hurled his javelins bright,
Till all the ether seemed aglow
    With flames of rapid flight.
The Genii's Sultan found the fire
    Surpassed his utmost force,
And, darting lightnings in his ire,
    Was baffled in his course:
The dragon's wings compelled his might
    To yield, and in dismay
He turned his head to wildly smite
    The monster from his way.

207

The Elf King launched a magic dart,
　That smote his fiery eyes,
And, blinded by this potent art,
　He fled the fatal skies :
His Afrites then retreated slow
　Before the elves and gnomes,
Whose dragon steeds, with wondrous glow,
　Now saved their mountain homes :
They drove the endless legions back
　With fierce, relentless sweep,
And deadly flames illumed their track :
　Till, near the ocean deep,
The Genii sought their cloudy camp,
　When, by their King's command,
A truce was sounded, ere the lamp
　Of day had left the land.

The victors met in conclave now :
　The Elfin King foretold,

THE QUEEN OF THE FAIRIES.

That, on the morrow, when their vow
   Of truce no more would hold
Its virtue, battle, dark and grim,
   Should well be waged anew:
And Nature's powers would succor him:
   The ocean, deep and blue,
Arrayed in fearful tidal-wave,
   Should then the Genii whelm:
And soon the seas would wildly rave,
   Where glittered spear and helm.

The morning broke, the truce was o'er;
   While now the blinded King
Displayed his Genii on the shore,
   With haughty crest and wing:
He bade the host, his sceptre swayed,
   Storm every height with spears:
But, at a signal, part should aid
   Their valorous compeers

By rising in the air, despite
    The dragons' dangerous power.
And, sweeping round with rapid flight.
    Should reach the fairies' bower.
The Afrites moved like whirlwinds on:
    But suddenly the plain
Became a lake of fire: anon,—
    While yet, with fierce disdain,
They braved the fiery waves that rose
    To whelm them in their course,
And, breathing storms around their foes.
    Used every dread resource,—
There came across the mighty sea
    A tidal-wave sublime,
That rose, by Nature's proud decree,
    To ravage that fair clime:
It grandly rolled, with crest of foam
    And mane of surges wild,
With awful force, from tempests' home,
    Like mountains skyward piled.

THE QUEEN OF THE FAIRIES.

And struck the island where the fire
 Rolled down to meet the deep;
Then, rising in majestic ire,
 With thundering roll and sweep,
Encountered that vast sea of flame
 In all unheard-of strife,
Till scalding vapours overcame
 The Genii's courage rife.
They fled before the fiery surge,
 And sought a distant shore,
To shun this all-destructive scourge,
 And meet such foes no more.
The Elf King's art protected well
 The Fairy Queen's domain,
And, by his potent ban and spell,
 The surges strove in vain
To reach the bloomy region where
 The fays securely dwelt,
Unharmed by all the powers of air,
 Though strange alarm they felt.

211

Throughout the day they watched the heights,
　　Or gazed across the sea
To catch the gleam of signal lights
　　From gnomes, that they might flee.
Beyond the mountain range they heard
　　The roar of onset wild,
And saw the flames the summits gird,
　　Where elves the foe beguiled :
But when the distant ocean rose
　　With terrors unforeseen,
Though surging billows whelmed their foes,
　　They feared their foaming sheen.
The charming Queen implored the Fire,
　　Within a temple grand,
And prayed to quell the Genii's ire,
　　That sought to spoil the land :
Her subjects thronged around the shrine,
　　To join their prayers to save
The mystic realm, of bliss divine,
　　From that appalling wave :

"Ye Powers supreme," they wildly sang.
　"Watch o'er this dreadful scene,
Protect our country from the clang
　Of arms, and rise between
The tide and our dear city fair,
　Where joy and peace abound,
Lest cruel anguish and despair
　In fairy-land be found!"
On pinions bright a vision came,
　Resplendent from the field,
To breathe the tale, that waves and flame
　Had made the Genii yield:
"The noble Kings have saved the day;"
　It cried, "the foe has fled;
And soon, in joyous, proud array,
　Shall sound our armies' tread:
They come, in conquest's joyful hour,
　Triumphant from the fray:
Then let your praise resound in power,
　And bless their ranks to-day!"

213

The pearly city rang its bells
   With joy for victory won:
Like insects swarming from their cells,
   The fays extolled the sun
That shone upon such conquering arms:
   And sylphs prepared to meet
The heroes whom their Sovereign's charms
   Inspired: the magic fleet
Sailed up to land the gnomes, who hailed
   Their Monarch's wondrous power:
That had by raging flames availed,
   In peril's darkest hour,
To crush the dreaded Genii's might:
   They blessed the Elf King, too,
Whose wisdom put the foe to flight,
   And Nature's secrets knew.
The Court moved on, along the tide,
   To meet the warriors bold:
While gnomes and fays in songs replied,
   The paths were strewn with gold:

214

THE QUEEN OF THE FAIRIES.

The Fairy Queen was borne in state
    To greet the allied Kings
Who saved her from such direful fate:
    And hope illumed her wings;
For well she saw the Elf King prized
    Her radiant beauty rare,
And, blushing deep, she now surmised,
    His love she well could share.
With sound of trumpets came the troops,
    In pageantry and pride,
And marched along the fairy groups,
    That each in blessings vied:
While, in a car by griffins drawn,
    Advanced the Elfin King,
Who, those fierce days, from early dawn,
    Had never ceased to bring
New forces boldly into play;
    And, by his brilliant power,
Had been the hero of each day
    In battle's wildest hour.

The Elf King met the lovely Queen.
    Who crowned his valiant brow
With choicest laurel wreaths: his mien
    Was glorious; and now
He smiled as heroes only can,
    And prayed her be his bride.
The Queen rejoiced, and soon began
    To shape, with virgin pride.
A noble answer: then a blush
    Adorned her beauteous face,
As, low and sweet, she whispered: "Hush!
    I grant thee. King, thy grace."
The meteor chariots rose in state
    To gain the palace height,
Where gathered soon those Monarchs great,
    In victors' pomp and might:
Through jewelled panes, of every hue,
    A splendor filled the hall,
Where opal columns met the view,
    And emerald thrones for all!

THE QUEEN OF THE FAIRIES.

A dragon sped across the wave
   To bring the Pontiff grand:
Who came, upon that fiery slave,
   To bless this fairy-land:
He brought, with sylphids in their train,
   The Queen that ruled the gnomes.
And that sweet Fay who could disdain
   A crown, from joyous homes.
The bridal pageant decks the eve,
   Winged legions hover bright
Where mountain crests and towers receive
   A panoply of light;
The golden domes all beaming glow,
   While palaces aspire
To blaze with diadems, and show
   Weird battlements of fire.
The Pontiff blessed the Royal pair
   Before the brilliant Court,
And then, while incense filled the air,
   The tranquil sea they sought:

A magic bark, with diamond oars,
    Awaits the lovers twain,
Who leave the dazzling, golden shores
    To cross the peaceful main.
The Tritons blow the nuptial horn,
    And, riding dolphins proud,
With torches red their course adorn,
    Until, from veil of cloud,
The moon bursts out in radiance mild,
    And silvers o'er the deep,
While sounds a fairy music wild,
    That lulls the waves to sleep.
They float away to palmy isles,
    Where raptured hours will fly,
While Elfin glory, bliss beguiles,
    Beneath the tropic sky.

THE OCEAN.

A SONG OF TRIUMPH.

My iceberg fleet ne'er knew defeat!
   The boundless Ocean cried,
Like castled rocks, they breast the shocks
   Of my advancing tide;
I float their spires in sunset fires
   That gild the toppling chain;
Like emeralds' shine, their glorious line
   Adorns my swelling main:
The glittering heights, like phantom knights,
   Watch o'er my gleaming rest,
Where glacial streams elude the beams
   That warm my sovereign breast:
The mariners fear the ice-fields drear,
   That crush the good ship's side,
While cloud and mist obedient list,
   And stars refuse to guide;—

THE OCEAN.

But weary grown I claim my own,
   And sink the monsters dread,
Though storm and sun have scarce begun
   To woo each giant head.
My rivers cold are grandly rolled
   To soothe the Tropics' glow ;
And cheer the isles, enwreathed in smiles,
   Where gales of spices blow :
While palm trees bend, and greetings send,
   In verdant majesty,
Flows, swift and wide, my balmy tide,
   To thrill each Polar sea.

Night soars to wield her radiant shield,
   I rise, entranced, to greet,
And silvery waves array as slaves
   For Dian's chaste retreat :
She is my Queen ! with ardent mien
   I follow, as she flies ;

A SONG OF TRIUMPH.

Her splendors bright my course invite,
   Beneath the dazzling skies.
When waked to bliss by Apollo's kiss
   My vapours mount on high,
They spurn the Earth in celestial mirth,
   And snow-clad peaks defy :
Where glaciers glow, floods sweep below,
   As flames the meteor star ;
Like angels' flight, these dreams of light
   Salute my surge afar.

My throne I rear where sailors fear
   Nor storm nor whirlwind wild,
Sublime expanse defies the glance
   Of lightning—tempest's child :
There, islands gem my diadem,
   While far I spread my sway
In mighty seas more wild than these,
   That continents obey.

THE OCEAN.

My fearless arms invoke the charms
    The fierce tornado weaves;
I joy in storms' majestic forms,
    Though peace my bosom leaves:
I love the cyclone of the Torrid Zone,
    And arise in robes of pride
With a crown of spray, till the King of Day
    Is hidden beneath my tide:
I lash the strand, and assail the land
    With crested legions vast,
While breakers rave, and the thundering wave
    Is hurled before the blast.
I hail the fires of Vulcan's pyres.
    And pour my torrents in
To raging rise and brave the skies
    When Titan wars begin.
The globe is mine, with power divine
    Around the world I roll,
And wield a might from realms of light
    To each ice-guarded pole!

A LEGEND OF VESUVIUS.

I.

A maiden stood on Capri's isle,
And watched, with soft, ingenuous smile,
    The wavelets throbbing beat;
Where rolled, with slow, majestic sweep,
The surges of the classic deep
    That glowed beneath her feet.

II.

"Vesuvius is lulled to rest,"
    She murmured; "if the saints arrest
        The dreadful mountain's power,
No more we'll view on yonder shore
The fiery torrents raging pour,
        All Nature to devour."

A LEGEND OF VESUVIUS.

III.

A throng of merry peasants came
To where she watched the morning flame
    Beneath Aurora's tread;
They paused beside a ruined pile,
With tambourine, and danced the while
    The dawn's red glories fled.

IV.

The Tarantella's merry sound
Re-echoed from the hills around,
    As many a dancer vied,
In joyous bounds, with light gazelle;
While gallant swains would fondly tell
    Where stood the island's pride.

V.

The maiden whom they honored so
Enjoyed the early morning's glow;
    She cared not for the dance;
Her fancy soared beyond the sphere
She sweetly filled: no youth was dear
    For whom she deigned a glance.

VI.

The young Antonio hopeless viewed
The charmer who his will subdued;
    Teresa would not smile
On his impetuous, wayward zeal;
And oft he, raging, stamped his heel,
    And cursed his want of guile.

VII.

Then, in the dance's wildest whirl
He plunged, to find no beauteous girl
  Could ever be compared
With this enchanting tyrant fair:
Whate'er his faults, he could not share
  The love his heart declared.

VIII.

He soon drew near the maiden fair,
And seemed to watch with envious air
  When breezes kissed her cheek,
Or fanned her glossy, raven locks;
Then clambered o'er the nearest rocks
  Her faintest smile to seek.

226

A LEGEND OF VESUVIUS.

IX.

" Why looks Teresa on the bay,
  Nor joins the dance, the livelong day?"
    He whispered, half in jest.
The thoughtful maiden answered not,
And soon Antonio left the spot
    With burning in his breast.

X.

Across the lovely bay she viewed,
As though a dream its flight pursued,
    A brilliant pageant glide;
Where gilded barges seemed to shine
In long and glittering, golden line,
    That graced the sparkling tide.

A LEGEND OF VESUVIUS.

XI.

"The conquering Normans come again,"
She sighed, " and now these worst of men
   The Pope a captive lead :
What means this regal pageantry?
And whither can we vainly flee?
   May Heaven our terrors heed!"

XII.

The wondrous bay, in glory's pride,
Now glowed in sunlight, as the tide
   Rolled up the rocky strand
Where dark Vesuvius frowning stood,
With vineyards clad o'er many a rood,
   But threatening the land.

XIII.

The stately argosy drew near,
And soon she dashed away a tear;
   For, on a gorgeous prow,
A monarch's diadem was seen
To shine, the courtier ranks between,
   Upon a noble brow.

XIV.

"Is this King Roger?" said the maid,
"That warrior bold, who armies swayed
   When Holy Mother Church
Compelled him to resign the realm
He won by force? that royal helm
   Deserved his anxious search."

A LEGEND OF VESUVIUS.

XV.

'T was Naples' King who sought the isle,
His cares of state to soothe awhile
   On Capri's dreamy shore :
Where glows an azure grot divine,
Like sapphires in a silver mine,
   Beyond the surges' roar.

XVI.

The maiden oft admired the cave
That gleams beside the dancing wave :
   She watched, with anxious thought,
As, through the grotto's low-browed arch,
While hautboys played a gallant march,
   The King its wonders sought.

XVII.

Beside the Monarch sat a youth,
Who chained her, by his look of truth
   And manly courage bold:
The diadem soon lost its charm,
For love awoke a new alarm,
   With visions bright, untold.

XVIII.

The handsome knight who won her gaze,
Until she felt a sweet amaze,
   Was clad in shining mail:
His helmet on a cushion lay,
And, as they glided o'er the bay,
   His voice entranced the gale.

231

A LEGEND OF VESUVIUS.

XIX.

Within the grotto's azure walls
The Monarch on each courtier calls
    For roundelay and song;
But when young Carlo's voice resounds,
The cavern seems to lose its bounds,
    As echoes, answering, throng.—

XX.

Antonio seeks Teresa's face,
He sees her blush, with winsome grace,
    As sweeps the pageant by;
While all the peasants rush to view
The King, as, o'er the waters blue,
    Like birds, the barges fly.

A LEGEND OF VESUVIUS.

XXI.

The Royal party brave a height
That frowns to dare the billows' might:
    And gaze across the foam
To where Vesuvius warns the gay,
That judgment sits beside the bay,
    Though beauty gilds each home.

XXII.

A towering cloud is seen to rise,
Like Eblis challenging the skies,
    While hoarse the mountain roars:
The Norman turns to seek his barge,
And hastes to quit the rocky marge
    That girds fair Capri's shores.

233

A LEGEND OF VESUVIUS.

XXIII.

The peasant maiden came to show
The speediest path to shores below:
    Her beauty charmed the King:
And, drawing off a costly gem,
He said: "My royal diadem
    Is worthier than this ring:

XXIV.

"But yet, fair maiden, wear the toy:
The world shall not thy peace annoy,
    Though kingly gifts be great."—
The knight beholds the lovely maid,
And love's sweet hopes his heart invade,
    That seal his early fate.

234

A LEGEND OF VESUVIUS.

XXV.

He gazed in rapture on a face
Where Nature lavished every grace,
    Till dawned a roseate hue,
All glowing, like the blush of morn:
From lustrous orbs, a glance of scorn
    The glittering bauble drew.

XXVI.

"Ah! had I only crossed the bay,"
He thought, "before this startling day,
    And that sweet maiden fair
Should then have blushed to see my face,
Or smiled, as now, with charming grace,—
    What would not lovers dare!

A LEGEND OF VESUVIUS.

XXVII.

"I might have dwelt with her alone;
The world had drifted on unknown
    To hearts as true as ours:
Or my good sword had won a throne,
Where she in beauty would have shone,
    Who strewed my path with flowers."

XXVIII.

The Monarch bids the maiden leave
Her native isle, nor fondly grieve
    If parents sigh in vain,
And follow with the brilliant Court;
That gleaming barks will soon transport
    To brave the fire's reign.

A LEGEND OF VESUVIUS.

XXIX.

The knight rejoiced to hear her doom ;
For now, he trusted, in the gloom
    That shrouded all the bay,
The lovely prize might fall his lot ;
And then the Church should tie the knot
    No king could rend away.

XXX.

"Sir Carlo ! " said the King, with pride,
" As down this rocky, mountain side,
    To reach the sea we go,
I charge thee, watch the maiden well ;
But guard thee from her witching spell
    And love's enchanting glow."

XXXI.

The knight obeyed his Monarch's will;
But fair Teresa, grieving still
    On quitting friends and home,
O'ercame his earnest, loyal thought:
And soon his heart all eager sought
    In kindred paths to roam.

XXXII.

"Perhaps," he dreamed, "the King will soon
Forget the maid, and, if the boon
    Be craved by gallant knight,
He yet may pardon if we fly:
At worst, a warrior can but die
    Though braving regal might."

A LEGEND OF VESUVIUS.

XXXIII.

Whate'er his ardent thoughts can shape,
The guards allow her no escape;
    And now the royal barge
Receives the maiden, weeping sore,
As from the island's rocky shore
    The sailors bear their charge.

XXXIV.

The peasants sadly gathered round
When King and guards had left the ground;
    Antonio stoutly said:
"I follow in my swiftest boat
Where'er these barges gay may float,
    Though it should cost my head!"

239

XXXV.

Like swallow skimming o'er the sea,
His boat then glances valiantly
   Along the golden waves;
Teresa gazes on the bark,
That follows toward the mountain dark,
   And every danger braves.

XXXVI.

The hapless maiden sighed to think,
Antonio would never shrink
   From aught to win his way:
"The gallant knight shall never know,"
She murmured, "why he haunts me so,
   Nor fears the King this day."

240

A LEGEND OF VESUVIUS.

XXXVII.

While swiftly sped the barges' course,
And courtiers vied in laughter hoarse.
   The King observed the knight,
And saw he oft admired the maid,
As though some saint appeared arrayed
   In fair, celestial light.

XXXVIII.

The haughty Norman said: "Beware!
Brave warrior, know that none can share
   That smile except thy King:
Sweet maid, why seem so pensive now?
King Roger yet will deck thy brow,
   And bid thee gaily sing."

A LEGEND OF VESUVIUS.

XXXIX.

Teresa raised her lovely eyes,
And trembling with renewed surprise
    Replied: "Dread Monarch, grace!
Permit a happy, dreamy maid
To seek again the island shade
    Where dwells her fearless race."

XL.

The warriors laughed to hear her plea,
And, gazing on the murmuring sea,
    She longed to end her woe
By plunging 'neath the waters bright;
But thoughts of Carlo soothed her fright,
    And dreams of Eden's glow.

A LEGEND OF VESUVIUS.

XLI.

Across the bay the pageant flies,
And soon proud Naples' towers arise,
　　Illumed by ruddy gleam.
The courtiers land; and then in haste
The Monarch seeks the dreary waste
　　Where lava currents stream.

XLII.

A haughty zeal compels his grace
To subjects, who the Norman race
　　Obey with loyal pride;
The lava threatens hamlets fair,
And thither swift he would repair,
　　To save them from its tide.

A LEGEND OF VESUVIUS.

XLIII.

Now, roars the mountain in its might,
While clouds of ashes hasten night,
    And veil the verdant scene;
The Monarch brings the lovely maid
To gaze where kings may seem afraid
    Of Nature's fiercest mien.

XLIV.

The fearless knight beguiles the way
With many a whispered roundelay,
    And tender, winning glance;
The maiden smiles on him alone;
What youth, without a heart of stone,
    Would leave her fate to chance!

XLV.

While wings of darkness veiled the noon,
Antonio moored his bark, and soon
　　O'ertook the loving pair;
Then wondered at Teresa's smile,
Till cruel pangs he felt the while,
　　Aroused by jealous care.

XLVI.

At length the wished-for moment came,
When, gazing at the sea of flame,
　　The courtiers watched no more:
For well the knight had wooed the maid,
And, favored by the gathering shade,
　　They sought the distant shore.

245

XLVII.

"Can we but gain the sea," the knight
Soft whispered in their hasty flight,
   "A skiff will bear away,
To distant climes from danger free,
Two hearts that purest ecstasy
   Attunes this bridal day."

XLVIII.

Teresa, smiling, gave a glance
For which a knight would break a lance
   In charge at tourney grim ;
But soon the terrors of the day
O'ercame her hopes, for strength gave way-
   She closer clung to him.

XLIX.

"My Carlo, leave me here to die:"
She murmured, "'t is in vain we fly:
    And how could I atone
For bringing pain and grief on thee?
Ah, had I sunk in yonder sea,
    I should have died alone!"

L.

The knight reproved her with a kiss:
And, stooping down, replied: "Let this
    Restore your courage true:"
With that, he bore her in his arms:
Though steep the way, Teresa's charms
    Aroused his powers anew.

A LEGEND OF VESUVIUS.

LI.

He soon consoled his blooming bride,
And vowed that never from her side
    Should he be torn away:
Then, down the mountain's rugged steep,
They sought the glowing, azure deep
    And scenes of brighter day.

LII.

Meanwhile, the peasants wildly pray
The King to save their loved array
    Of happy household joys,
As onward sweeps the molten tide,
And, spreading, raging far and wide,
    The vineyards' wealth destroys.

LIII.

The Norman missed his lovely prize,
And fury glanced from Royal eyes :
　　He sought the pair in vain ;
Until, at length, he saw the knight—
'Mid flashes of the fiery light—
　　Descending to the plain.

LIV.

He bears the charming maiden fair ;
But love heroic, fierce despair
　　And knightly deeds are vain :
The Monarch's faithful guards arrest
Their flight while hastening to be blest
　　With Hymen's mystic chain.

249

A LEGEND OF VESUVIUS.

LV.

Antonio led the winding way
By which the guards o'ertook their prey;
    For, mad with jealous rage,
He only thought to seize the knight,
And, aiding her to hasty flight,
    The maiden's love engage.

LVI.

Young Carlo draws his trusty blade,
And fights to shield the trembling maid, —
    For well he knows the King:
But what can single courage do?
He soon is seized, and fettered too
    With chains the vassals bring.

A LEGEND OF VESUVIUS.

LVII.

"Teresa!" said the valiant knight,
"I die before the close of night—
   No pardon 'waits my eyes;
Such love as ours will bloom again,
But not amid the haunts of men—
   We meet in distant skies!"

LVIII.

The maiden, fainting, scarcely knew
Her fate: for, as brave Carlo drew
   His sword to guard his bride,
She swooned, till soldiers gently bore
The damsel fair, to weep before
   The King her knight defied.

A LEGEND OF VESUVIUS.

LIX.

In vain she prayed the Norman's grace:
He praised the beauty of her face;
    Then bade his courtiers stay
Antonio for the service done;
But he had vanished, and begun
    A wanderer's life that day.

LX.

The King surveyed the knight with scorn,
While sword and spurs were from him torn:
    He ordered willing slaves
To hurl him from the lofty height—
While raged Vesuvius in its might—
    Amid the fiery waves!

A LEGEND OF VESUVIUS.

LXI.

The maiden viewed the dreadful scene:
Then, springing up with frenzied mien,
    She sought her lover's fate;
And, leaping from the mountain's crest,
Perchance was wafted to the blest
    That enter Heaven's gate!

LXII.

When raves Vesuvius in the night,
The peasants whisper, with affright,
    That spirits haunt the scene:
A maiden calls across the gloom,
And meets, beside their fiery tomb,
    A youth of gallant mien.

ODE TO A COMET.

I.

Fair herald from the radiant spheres!
Sublime thy starry front appears,
    Adorned with silvery flame:
Thy train resplendent shoots afar
Like magic veil, or fairies' car
    When Merlin's legions came.

II.

Is thy bright mission fraught with peace?
And shall her tranquil sway increase?
    'T would seem an olive bough
That gleams in light across the sky,
More fair than palm of victory,
    As Night illumes thy brow.

ODE TO A COMET.

III.

What tidings from celestial halls
Are graven on thy scroll, that calls
    For Magian eyes to read?
The burning orb that bids thee on
Shall send its greetings proud, anon.
    The seraph host to lead.

IV.

Thy flaming sword betokens woe
To hapless nations: wondrous glow
    Is wreathed around the blade
That shimmers in the trembling North:
Shall battle's trumpets summon forth
    Pale Strife, by thee arrayed?

ODE TO A COMET.

V.

Thy streamers seek the zenith bright,
Like flashes of the Northern light,
    With weird, imperial sweep;
While, hastening to the Western sea,
Thy banner, floating wild and free,
    Shall crest the mighty deep.

VI.

Dread standard of Eternity!
Since boundless space is naught to thee,
    What distant starry clime
Shall next salute thy dazzling whirl,
And see thee plunge where flames unfurl
    Suns' canopies sublime?

ODE TO A COMET.

VII.

Farewell, majestic beacon-glow!
Celestial rivers beaming flow
   To greet thy mystic ray:
Soar flashing through the realms of night,
While stars exert their giant might
   To bend thee to their sway.

VIII.

If, circling round our destined home
In shining worlds, thy star may roam
   And meet our raptured gaze,
Soft gleams of Paradise thy train,
We yet may hail that radiant chain
   Amid the Heavenly maze.

A ROMANCE OF AMALFI.

———

I.

How fair a spot the dreamy grot
   That overlooks the sea,
Where quaint Amalfi's ancient towers
Arise from bloomy orange-bowers,
   That wreathe her mountains free !

II.

When moonbeams glow o'er seas below,
   Fond lovers seek the place
To watch the silver orb divine
Adorn the waves, that softly shine
   In lines of trembling grace.

A ROMANCE OF AMALFI.

III.

A charming maid oft sought its shade,
　　To pray before the cross
That spreads its arms to lead the soul
To rise and seek the heavenly goal,
　　Forgetting mortal loss.

IV.

She chose an hour when spirits' power
　　Could not disturb her prayer;
For early eve serenely smiled
As she her lonely way beguiled
　　With hymns to soothe her care.

V.

She mourned a youth she loved in sooth,
　　Who rudely had been torn
From fondest friends by corsairs bold,
And, o'er the sapphire waters, sold
　　For Moorish beck and scorn.

259

VI.

A daring knight, with raptured sight,
    Oft watched the beauteous maid,
As, charmed, she turned her liquid eyes
To view the sunset leave the skies
    In gorgeous hues arrayed :

VII.

With flowers he strewed the craggy road
    Where'er her steps would glide,
While oft the sound of sweet guitar
Awoke the slumbering rocks afar,
    And cheered the mountain side.

VIII.

Bianca's home beside the foam
    With every grace was decked ;
Her tower looked across the deep,
As though the stones would vigils keep
    Where all her hopes were wrecked.

IX.

Luigi dwelt where mountains melt
  To clouds of fleecy white ;
But oft the gallant lover came
To fan what seemed a hopeless flame
  And watch her footsteps light.

X.

Devotion vain could never gain
  A glance from her he sought ;
She dreamed of burning sands away,
Where captives sighed the dreary day,
  While tasks severe they wrought.

XI.

The years rolled by, a foreign sky
  By him she loved was owned,
Who, weary of this lonely lot,
Had ne'er his native land forgot,
  Where friends his fate bemoaned :

XII.

At length despair increased his care,
　　Till, longing to be free.
He cast away his early creed,
To find himself, from prison freed,
　　A rover of the sea.

XIII.

He joined a band that left the land
　　For plunder o'er the foam;
The corsair crew no pity knew.
And swiftly o'er the waters flew.
　　That bathed his early home.

XIV.

His valor won a fight. begun
　　With ships from Venice fair:
And now the chieftain he was named,
While Terror's accents oft proclaimed,
　　That ruin was his care.

XV.

Amalfi's shore re-echoed o'er
 The name he newly bore,—
For Angelo was Ali called,—
And mothers' hearts grew more appalled
 As redder grew his score.

XVI.

With knightly tread, Luigi led
 A valiant hero band
To watch the coast when ships appeared,
Lest rovers, like the chief they feared,
 Should boldly strive to land.

XVII.

The corsairs sought,—whene'er they fought,
 And won a golden prize
Along Salerno's gulf,—to hide
Their booty in the ruins wide
 Where Paestum's shafts arise.

263

XVIII.

A gallant fleet had met defeat,
    And, treasures vast their spoil.
They hastened to the lonely scene,
Where Neptune's columns rise between
    The shrines, to crown their toil.

XIX.

A distant blaze soon met their gaze,
    For scouts had warned the land:
And now Luigi's warriors came,
A squadron bold, athirst for fame,
    To crush the Moslem band.

XX.

The corsair crew their weapons drew:
    While Ali's rampant zeal
Soon led them to assail the knight:
And yataghans shone fiercely bright,
    Destructive blows to deal.

XXI.

To guard their coast, the Christian host
   Charged bravely on the foe:
Their war-cry sounded loud and true,
And deadly javelins gleaming flew
   To lay the Moslem low.

XXII.

Luigi sought where Ali fought
   With scimitar and shield,
And, raising high his noble sword,
Smote down the leader of the horde,
   Whose blood soon dyed the field.

XXIII.

With furious strife to save his life,
   The corsairs thronged around,
Till many a Christian knight and squire,
With cloven helm and rich attire,
   Lay slain upon the ground.

265

A ROMANCE OF AMALFI.

XXIV.

The Moslems then, like gallant men,
    Retreated to the shore :
They bore brave Ali in their arms,
While many muttered mystic charms
    To soothe his wounds the more.

XXV.

Luigi's band, along the strand,
    Maintained a stubborn fight,
Until the corsairs launched their bark,
And, favored by the evening dark,
    Succeeded in their flight.

XXVI.

The wounded chief now found relief,
    Yet hovered near the shore,
Resolved to greet the charming face
That lent his youthful dreams their grace,
    If fate would smile once more.

A ROMANCE OF AMALFI.

XXVII.

His dauntless crew impatient grew,
　　Till leaving them, unknown,
A slender skiff, he chose for speed,
Soon bore him where a daring deed
　　Might make the maid his own.

XXVIII.

The Christians saw the Moors withdraw,
　　Then hastened home with joy,
Displaying trophies bravely won:
Salerno triumphed like the sun,
　　And blessed their grand employ.

XXIX.

Amalfi hailed her warriors mailed;
　　Luigi's name was sung
Throughout the land, and damsels vied
With knights in greeting him with pride,
　　While garlands gay they flung.

XXX.

Bianca smiled, her cares beguiled
    By tales of knightly deeds,
And praised Luigi's valor true:
While brightly winged the hours flew,
    Like bees o'er flowery meads.

XXXI.

At eve she sought the grotto, wrought
    To tears by happy dreams:
But, mindful of her early love,
Soon turned her wandering thoughts above
    To stars' mysterious beams:

XXXII.

" While 'neath the sky his course may lie,
    Who won my girlish heart,
My faith will hope for meeting yet:
Perhaps when life's bright star has set,"
    She dreamed, " we ne'er shall part."

268

XXXIII.

What rustled then along the glen?
　　She started in surprise:
For Moorish robes and turban light
Appeared to mock her wondering sight,
　　And Ali met her eyes:

XXXIV.

"Fair Bianca, see! I come to thee,
　　'T is Angelo that speaks!"
The corsair murmured: wild with grief
She gazed upon the haughty chief,
　　And tears bedewed her cheeks.

XXXV.

"Restore thy gold, thou corsair bold,"
　　She sighed, "and let me fly:
I loved young Angelo the brave:
But thou, a renegade and slave:
　　Ah, rather would I die!"

269

XXXVI.

"Come, Bianca love, the stars above,"
    He whispered, "smile for thee :
Oh fly with me across the foam :
There waits a happy, distant home,
    Where palms adorn the sea !"

XXXVII.

"Thy wounds betray the recent fray,"
    She answered through her tears.
"If Christian blood hath stained thy sword,
No happiness could love afford :
    I shrink with maiden fears.

XXXVIII.

"Oh change thy life, and cease from strife :
    I never can be thine :
Forget the past, and look on high :
Perhaps in yonder radiant sky
    We'll meet by power divine !"

XXXIX.

The corsair gazed, as though amazed,
 Then bent to seize his prey:
Bianca shrieked, and lo! the knight
Appeared before the grotto's height,
 And held the Moor at bay.

XL.

Luigi's blade her prayer obeyed,
 And spared the wounded foe:
While Angelo's remorse began
To shape his life with altered plan:
 He sought a shrine below.

XLI.

The knight and maid now left the shade
 To reach her lonely tower:
Luigi vowed his love so well,
Bianca's blush alone could tell
 How true she felt his power.

271

A ROMANCE OF AMALFI.

XLII.

Amalfi's knight, who gained the fight,
    Was worthy deemed by all :
While rivals envied such a lot,
Luigi's prowess, ne'er forgot,·
    Their plaudits would recall.

XLIII.

He bore his bride, in joyous pride,
    To dwell beside a stream
That murmured round his ancient towers :
While orange-groves arrayed their flowers
    To make her life a dream.

XLIV.

They wandered o'er the pebbly shore,
    And often sought the grot
Where he had guarded her so well;
Then oft, transported, he would tell
    How he had gained the spot.

XLV.

One eve they saw, with reverent awe,
    A monk absorbed in prayer.
Who told his beads with raptured eyes,
As, gazing on the starry skies,
    He sought forgiveness there.

XLVI.

'T was Angelo that knelt below
    The grotto's dreamy height:
For cloister-walls had bent his pride,
And naught he sought on earth beside
    A pilgrim's path of light.

XLVII.

The grotto's shrine seemed half divine,
    As moonlight decked the sea:
The pilgrim felt the heavens near:—
Then Bianca shed a silent tear,
    For Angelo was free.

THE TAKING OF NEW ORLEANS.

I.

O stately live-oaks' verdant guise,
And orange groves, where Southern skies
O'er madly rushing floods arise,
    Ye breathe of war's sublimity!

II.

Armed ramparts ruled the river wide,
And mail-clad vessels swept the tide,
Forbidding Freedom's flag to ride
    The glorious Mississippi.

274

III.

A valiant fleet displayed its might,
And swift the sunbeams turned to night
With smoke, illumed by rockets bright
    And flash of many a battery:

IV.

Though fire-ships came flaming down,
The Commodore, with dauntless frown.
Advanced to seize the distant town,
    While roared the cannon threatening:

V.

The glowing shells, with lightning gleams,
Like meteors hurled in fiery streams,
Assailed his ships, they crowned with beams
    Of radiant immortality:

VI.

With hearts as staunch as knights of old,
The sailor warriors, true and bold,
Where battle's heaviest thunders rolled,
    Swept thro' the shells' wild hurricane.

VII.

With awful strife a fleet was won;
The forts then ceased to cloud the sun;
At length, the crash of booming gun
    No longer thrilled in majesty.

VIII.

But now, when quiet reigns supreme,
We tell the story like a dream,
How Farragut, by fort and stream,
    His heroes led to victory!

THE CHAMOIS HUNTER.

I.

The Rhone leaps down where mountains frown,
　　Like Titans, round her glacier spring,
While, far below the glittering snow,
　　Her ripples flash on rainbow wing.

II.

O wondrous height of gleaming light,
　　Where chamois hunters gaily leap,
Thy icy breast affords no rest
　　For those thy arms would fondly keep!

277

III.

The chamois seeks the lofty peaks;
  There winter's reign is never o'er;
Yet hunters brave the frozen wave,
  And reach where man ne'er climbed before.

IV.

Though storm winds fought, young Albert sought
  The crags for that exciting chase;
His valor reft the Alps, and left
  The antelope no resting-place.

V.

The rapid flood oft stirred his blood,
  Where Aar's blithe river plunges down;
And, standing near the torrent clear,
  He dreamed his love deserved a crown.

278

VI.

For chains his heart endured, apart
   From her he hoped to call his own,
And oft her name in echoes came,
   When wandering near the rushing Rhone.

VII.

A rival dwelt where glaciers belt
   Fair Grindelwald's romantic vale;
He wooed the maid whose heart obeyed
   The power of Albert's whispered tale:

VIII.

Her modest home rose near the foam
   Of Staubbach's veil of misty spray;
Like happy bird her songs were heard,
   With many a yodel's warble gay.

THE CHAMOIS HUNTER.

IX.

When moonlight shone o'er mountains lone,
  She wandered oft to see the snow
On Jungfrau's height reflect the light,
  In dazzling beams of silver glow.

X.

Brave Albert came her thoughts to claim
  By deep devotion, and to bring
The spoils he won 'neath burning sun,
  And hear fair Margaret sweetly sing.

XI.

He urged his suit, but she was mute,
  Although she felt his wondrous power:
For Rudolph's love appeared above
  His comrade's in the evening hour.

XII.

When Rudolph said his fate he read,
　And praised the youth who won her heart,
Within her eyes a sweet surprise
　Betrayed a love too deep for art.

XIII.

He strove to tell, whate'er befell
　His early dreams, he fain would live
Where he might hear her footsteps cheer
　The way, since hope she could not give.

XIV.

Well Albert knew his rival flew
　Across the Wengern Alp, like bird,
To greet the maid, whose charms arrayed
　New strife, where'er her name was heard.

281

THE CHAMOIS HUNTER.

XV.

By daring deed, each sought to lead
  Her heart to dwell on him alone;
And told of peaks, that blanched her cheeks,
  Where eagle's wing had scarcely flown.

XVI.

Each gladsome day they chased their prey
  Where Alps, 'mid glacier seas, arise
With icy spires, like Gothic choirs,—
  Cathedrals of the mighty skies.

XVII.

Their steps were true, though dangers grew,
  In bounding o'er the vast crevasse,
While up the steep, like chamois' leap,
  They scaled the snowy mountain pass.

THE CHAMOIS HUNTER.

XVIII.

She heard their tale, nor could avail
  Her prayers to tempt them to refrain,
Although a smile would oft beguile
  Her thoughts to dream these fears were vain.

XIX.

The Jungfrau's crown of snow looks down
  To woo the traveller's heart to climb
Where, veiled in white, her dangerous height
  Is decked as though the bride of Time.

XX.

Brave hearts must lead the course indeed
  Of those who seek the dizzy crest ;
There mountaineers, who smile at fears,
  Might dare the world the crags to breast.

THE CHAMOIS HUNTER.

XXI.

All-glorious peaks! the summer weeks
    Bring worshippers to view a shrine
Whose mountains bright are crowned with light,
    Like altars reared by might divine.

XXII.

Then silence reigns o'er crags and plains,
    As waiting for the full-voiced choir,
That bursts in power when tempests lower,
    And lightning strikes her thunder-lyre.

XXIII.

A daring band had reached the land
    Where avalanches crashing roll,
To climb, with zest, the shining crest
    The Jungfrau wears to fire the soul:

284

XXIV.

Her wondrous miles of gleaming wiles
   Extend, like giant arms, to greet
With dread caress whoe'er address
   Their might to rise like chamois fleet.

XXV.

At break of morn, the Alpine horn
   Aroused the echoes rolling wide,
And clouds gave way before the day,
   Whose glance adorned the valleys' pride.

XXVI.

The hunters came, with famous name,
   From many a glacier's icy fount,
To lead, where beam the heights supreme,
   The youths who sought the awful mount.

285

THE CHAMOIS HUNTER.

XXVII.

They clambered high, as though the sky
   Were what their courage strove to reach,
O'er ice and snow ; till far below
   Rose heights that late incited each.

XXVIII.

A cord, entwined, their strength combined,
   And Albert boldly climbed the way ;
His face shone bright in danger's sight,
   While all obeyed his gallant sway.

XXIX.

He bravely led o'er ice-fields dread,
   With merry heart and kindling eye,
Rejoiced to show the realms of snow,
   That glowed beneath the azure sky.

THE CHAMOIS HUNTER.

XXX.

With bold device, he cleft the ice,
   Till diamond steps appeared to rise
To lead the brave where genii rave
   When mortals press so near the skies.

XXXI.

The day was bright, yet snow-flakes light
   Half veiled a terrible crevasse:
He bounding said : " With hunter's tread,
   A valiant heart may safely pass."

XXXII.

Beyond arose the heights that close
   The glaciers' path with icy stairs :
A gay, young count, who spurns the mount,
   Is lost amid these fearful snares :

XXXIII.

A shriek! a cry from kinsmen nigh :
   The cord is strangely cut in twain :—
The deep crevasse receives a mass
   Of struggling youths, who shout in vain :

XXXIV.

The Alpine sprites with mystic lights
   Illumed the chasm as they fell :
Or 't was the ray the king of day
   Threw down to loose each magic spell.

XXXV.

The chief was spared, while Rudolph dared
   To rend the cord to save his life :—
Like raging fire was Albert's ire ;
   He cursed the use of caitiff knife.

THE CHAMOIS HUNTER.

XXXVI.

The strands gave way the instant they
 Had seized the ice to stay the fall;
But now he sought, with dauntless thought,
 To reach the grot and save them all:

XXXVII.

Let knotted cord its aid afford:
 Young Albert fastened one, with care,
He ever brought, by danger taught,
 And then swung boldly through the air.

XXXVIII.

Descending deep, the dreadful steep
 Soon towered o'er his noble head,
While emerald light shone ever bright
 Where ice-cliffs frowned above the dead:

289

THE CHAMOIS HUNTER.

XXXIX.

A gallant youth was crushed, in truth,
  And sadly round his form the rest
Awaited now, with anxious brow,
  Whate'er the leader deemed the best.

XL.

O heart at rest! a spirit blest
  Soars joyfully to starry realms:
In icy halls each thought recalls
  Thy crowns of worth, like knightly helms!

XLI.

When Albert gained the cavern, pained
  To hear the count had perished there,
He bade each friend, in turn, ascend,
  And scale the heights of upper air.

XLII.

The hapless corse, then left perforce,
    Secured by his heroic care,
They waft above with arms of love :—
    A woful burden 't is to bear.

XLIII.

The champion lone, more zealous grown,
    Now lingers, like the sunbeam's glow,
In sapphire sheen the cliffs between,
    Where heaven had dawned on one below ;

XLIV.

Then calls in turn to gladly learn
    That all is well ; and bids them fling
The trusty strands his fate demands,
    That he may, climbing, succor bring ;—

THE CHAMOIS HUNTER.

XLV.

But Rudolph dreamed his rival, deemed
  The bravest Swiss on glaciers wild,
Might bid them mark his treason dark ;
  And cruel thoughts his heart beguiled.

XLVI.

He hurled the cord : ere Albert soared,
  Like angel guarding those he saved :
What demon blade its power essayed ?
  The strands flew down the cliff he braved.

XLVII.

A cry of grief for their young chief
  Arose upon the sighing air :
All left in haste the icy waste,
  To call new aid and rescue there.---

THE CHAMOIS HUNTER.

XLVIII.

Adown the mount they bore the Count,
  While requiems were gently sung
By wailing winds. till mourners' minds
  With woful agony were wrung.

XLIX.

The storm clouds rose, like angry foes,
  To drive them from the dreary height;
Then raved the blast, and phantoms vast
  Swept by on wings of awful might:

L.

With thunder tones, from icy thrones,
  The avalanches, hurled in power,
O'ertook their flight to vales of light,
  Yet spared them in that dreadful hour:

THE CHAMOIS HUNTER.

LI.

While Rudolph showed new zeal, and glowed
    With hope that soon the maiden sweet
Might heed his prayer; the piercing air
    But seemed his eager thoughts to greet.

LII.

O Switzerland! the stalwart band
    The traitor led could not believe,
A son of thine, with base design,
    Would bid so many brothers grieve!

LIII.

They hastened then, like trusty men,
    With anxious hearts, to tell, alas!
How, far away, brave Albert lay
    A captive in a dread crevasse.

THE CHAMOIS HUNTER.

LIV.

The woful tale reached Margaret's vale :
    And swiftly as the deer she sped,
To urge along a hardy throng
    To save the youth, ere life had fled.

LV.

All clambered through the snow that flew
    As though to daunt their noble zeal :
The cord they bore might hover o'er
    A scene where Death had set his seal.

LVI.

But, joy untold ! a hunter bold
    Descended to that icy lair
To find the youth, unharmed in sooth,
    Ascending by a magic stair:

THE CHAMOIS HUNTER.

LVII.

The hero gained the summit,—trained
  To brave the glaciers' frozen tide.—
Rejoiced to think that danger's brink
  Might win his love to be his bride.

LVIII.

Fond Margaret smiled, by hope beguiled,
  And listened to his pleading tale ;
While Rudolph fled the Alps, to wed
  His life to trouble's angry gale.

LIX.

Where mountains gleam o'er lake and stream,
  The lovers reared a fair retreat :
While bright-winged Peace bade joys increase
  And sweet delight their bridal greet.

www.ingramcontent.com/pod-product-compliance
Lightning Source LLC
Chambersburg PA
CBHW020846020726
47497CB00005B/1274